Company
of Shadows

AIRSHIP 27 PRODUCTIONS

AN AIRSHIP 27 PRODUCTION

Company of Shadows
© 2019 Wayne Carey

Published by Airship 27 Productions
www.airship27.com
www.airship27hangar.com

Interior illustrations © 2019 Ed Catto
Cover illustration © 2019 Laura Givens

Editor: Ron Fortier
Associate Editor: Jaime Ramos
Marketing and Promotions Manager: Michael Vance
Production and design by Rob Davis

ISBN-13: 978-1-946183-53-8
ISBN-10: 1-946183-53-9

Printed in the United States of America

10 9 8 7 6 5 4 3 2 1

Company of Shadows

by Wayne Carey

Chapter One

For we are but of yesterday, and know nothing, because our days upon earth are a shadow... Job 8:9

The boom from the cannon rocked the valley, echoing across the hills.

The vibration traveled through the ground, through my body, and into my soul. A hundred birds took flight, crying out as they scattered. Half a mile away, the train whistle blew, announcing the train's approach. It chugged along the tracks that split the rolling fields on its way past the small clump of trees and shrubs that concealed our party. The six of us hunkered down behind the brush, with the young maples shading us from the relentless August sun. A pile of old ties further up and on the opposite side of the tracks hid men of Company H.

Next to me, Charlie chewed on a dried weed and craned his neck in an attempt to see the train. The weathered brim of his slouch hat hid his eyes. Next to him, Badger slipped off his battered kepi and used a stained red kerchief to wipe the sweat from his broad, bearded face. He shoved the cloth back into the pocket of his faded trousers, a wrinkled corner dangling out as he drew his hand away, then grunted as he crouched his bulk lower. Sam spat a wad of tobacco into the grass and wiped the stubble on his chin to rid his face of telltale spittle. Daniel cast him an annoyed look, then turned his dark eyes back toward the approaching train. Sunlight glinted off the round lenses of his spectacles. Beside me, Steve stared through the brush at the tracks in front of us. Sweat dribbled down his face in rivulets. His jaw was set in stern concentration, but his fingers tapped the shaft of his musket. He wet his lips with a pass of his tongue, wiped his mouth with the back of his hand, and resumed his nervous tapping. He was only seventeen years old, and here he was, crouched in hiding, about to take part in his first train raid.

Cannon thundered again, the sound rolling over the mountains rising at our backs.

The screech of protesting brakes pierced the humid air, and the train began its deceleration.

"Ready!" Badger yelled.

5

We stood straight and cocked our muskets.

"Aim!"

The train continued to slow as it passed our concealment. The faces of passengers peered out the windows. A heavy woman in a blue bonnet passed under my sights. Her wide eyes scanned the vegetation and caught sight of us now only partially hidden. I moved the barrel of my Enfield along the passenger cars, past women and children, until I found a man in a blue uniform. His pale face glared out at me and I felt his eyes pierce through me. Gold straps glistened on his shoulders. As I kept my aim on him, a smile curved his drooping mustache. He wasn't just looking out at the country side, he was looking directly at me, singling me out from among our troops, as though he could tell I had him under my sights.

"Fire!"came Badger's command.

Our weapons blasted in one thundering roar, louder than the cannon, stinging my ears. Muzzle flashes flared and smoke rolled out to make a haze that all but obliterated the train.

"Reload. Fire at will."

We each were able to get another shot off before the train rolled to a stop. As the smoke curled off on the breeze, I tried to locate the mustached officer. He was gone, his window empty.

Badger gave a call and led us on the double toward the train. We clambered up the steps into the middle car, amidst startled passengers. Sam, Daniel and Charlie headed toward the rear of the train. Badger led Steve and me forward. I trailed behind and glanced over the passengers. Between twenty to thirty men and women, with a smattering of assorted children, twisted in their seats to watch us as we made our way down the aisle. After the brightness of the sunlight outside, the passengers were shadowy figures in the gloomy interior of the train. Here sat the heavy-set woman in the blue bonnet, two small children with her. The others were civilians in all manner of dress. No military except for our group. The Union officer I had seen earlier was nowhere in the car.

Badger grabbed a woman's purse and rifled through it, then tossed it down on the seat beside her. He grunted. "Federal money. Ain't worth nothing here, lady."

A man started to rise, but Badger shook his head and lowered his musket in the man's general direction.

"Not a smart idea, sir. You got any gold?"

The passenger shook his head and eased himself down.

"Don't worry folks," I called out, catching everyone's attention. "We're just looking for some Federal soldiers with a strongbox. No one's going to get hurt as long as you don't interfere. Where'd the Union officer go? Let us know, then you can go about your business, enjoy the rest of your trip."

I leaned over the one seat toward the woman in the blue bonnet. "Where did that Union officer go, ma'am? He was right behind you when we stopped the train. Where is he?"

She shook her head, her plump cheeks wiggling. "Sir," she said in a soft Virginia accent, "there wasn't a soldier there. I saw two go through earlier, when the train first left the station, but I haven't seen one since."

Why, I wondered, would a good Southern lady lie about a Union officer?

I gave her a condescending smirk. "Now ma'am, I saw him."

"Well I did not," she said, clipping me off short. She patted her dress straight with a crinkle of starched petticoat and turned away with an annoyed "humph."

She had been looking out the window when the train had stopped, so she might not have been aware of the officer. Someone on the other side of the train might have seen him, or he might have gone toward the rear of the train, in which case Sam and the other men should have come across him. In the meantime, Badger headed toward the next car forward.

The darkness became oppressive, the car thick with shadows. When the train around me started to spin, I thought it had begun to move once more. We weren't supposed to be on board when it started back up and I wondered if we should try to jump off before it began to pick up speed, but that wasn't a very good plan. Then I realized that the train wasn't moving. There was no sound of the engine, no vibration through the floor of the car. My head was spinning. The heat was affecting me. This was summer, after all, and my cotton shirt beneath my wool shell jacket was soaked with sweat. I needed a drink before I passed out, so I fumbled for my canteen, pulling on the cloth strap slung over my shoulder. The chain on the cork caught on my haversack. I tugged the canteen free and fumbled with the cork. My hand shook as my fingers curled on the ring on the cork.

"They've got 'em!" Badger called from the far end of the car, where his bulk filled the door. A wide grin split his brown, gray-flecked beard as he pointed out a window to the left.

Steve ducked his head to look outside.

I gave up on the canteen and grabbed hold of the back of the nearest seat to hold onto the handle.

"Look!" a man seated on the left side said.

Passengers on the right stood. They bobbed their heads to see outside.

"Oh my," said the woman in the blue bonnet. She shoved past me to invade the seat opposite her, herding her two children like a hen with tiny chicks.

Passengers filled the aisle. A mass of shadows crowded around me, stealing the air and turning the atmosphere fetid. In the gloom, I tried to find Steve. Even Badger had been swallowed by the darkness.

But the outside was bright and I could plainly see men standing there. Six men in gray, four men in blue. Strangely, I could not recognize any of them.

One of those in blue was a lieutenant, the others privates. Two of these enlisted men carried a strongbox between them, its weight tugging down on their shoulders. A heavy lock kept the box shut. The third private carried a Springfield.

The men in gray wore tattered clothes covered in months of dirt and grime. They looked no older than teenagers under their filth. On two of them, their trousers were worn through at the knees. One of these men wore no shoes, his bare feet almost as black as the old brogans on the other men. One Confederate private had a weathered slouch hat covering his matted hair, the brim wilting down over his ears and the bridge of his hawk-like nose. In contrast, they carried new Sharps breech loaders, more common among Calvary units. The Confederate officer faired better than his men, or took better care to wash occasionally. A sweat stain encircled his slouch hat, but it still held its shape. His threadbare uniform was stained and bore no marks of his rank; his saber's scabbard was dented and scratched. He was an older man in his thirties, with a bushy mustache streaked with gray, and a dignified stance that hinted that he was used to giving orders. The Navy Colt in his right hand appeared clean and well cared for. He aimed it casually at the Federal lieutenant.

I couldn't hear their conversation, even though the windows were lowered to allow a meager breeze to flow through the car. The Confederate officer smiled, raising the ends of his mustache, and waved his Colt toward the strongbox. Three of his men chuckled. They lowered the barrels of their carbines at the Federal privates. The one Federal carrying the Springfield handed over his weapon to the closest Confederate. Another man stepped closer and slipped the private's bayonet out of its scabbard.

The lieutenant slowly lifted his own Colt from its holster and held it out, his fingers pinching the stock so that the pistol dangled with its barrel toward the ground. A Southern private snatched away the weapon.

The Confederate officer stretched out his arm, bringing his Colt to bear on the lieutenant's forehead.

I jumped at the explosion.

The lieutenant flew back, hurtling into the men holding the strongbox. The officer's head blew to pieces, bits of gore covering his men. The box thudded to the ground, his dead body sprawled over it.

Before the Federal privates could overcome their shock, carbines exploded. Blue coats blossomed with red, and the three soldiers crumpled to the ground.

Still grinning, the Confederate officer kicked the dead lieutenant in the side to topple him off the strongbox. Two of his men shouldered their carbines and took hold of the handles of the red-stained box.

No!

I tried to yell, to push my way through the crowd and shout out the window.

I stared at the body ... the boy lying on the tile floor, surrounded by a growing pool of blood. No, that wasn't right. This was outside. Bodies lay in the dirt. One man with his head blown apart. Three others lay around him.

The shadows inside the train car deepened, swallowing me up. I shivered in a sudden chill. It seemed as though I was in a frigid cavern deep in the earth, far away from any glimmer of sunlight. I needed to move, get outside, join my company, find out what was going on. No one was supposed to die. No one was supposed to shoot. They surrendered. They were prisoners. They were unarmed. And I couldn't shake the image of the dead boy, even though it had been a Federal officer who had been shot in the head. I kept seeing the young face explode as the pistol fired.

Fingers clasped around my arm.

"You okay?"

I turned to see Steve. A light sprang up from him, and the car brightened as though the overcast sky cleared before the bright summer sun. The chill dropped away from me and the heat under the wool of my shell jacket billowed outward.

"He's dead," I told Steve, "and I couldn't stop it." My own voice sounded distant. I wanted to tell him about the Union lieutenant lying in the dirt, but all I could think of, all I could see in my mind, was the boy lying on dirty tile, his life flowing from him.

Steve's mouth opened into a questioning circle, but he must not have been able to figure out what to ask. He looked out the window and I turned my head to follow his gaze.

Outside, the Confederates stood facing the Federals with the strongbox.

No one lay dead, no blood covered the grass and dirt.

Now I recognized the men in gray. Captain Jake Boden, waving his Colt at the Union lieutenant. Behind him were men of Company H, and joining them came Sam, Daniel, and Charlie, their muskets leveled menacingly. I even knew the men in blue, who were from the 46th Pennsylvania.

"Come on, Dad," Steve said. "We'll miss the ride back to camp."

I opened my mouth to tell him … tell him what? I wasn't sure. I had just seen four men murdered. I think. Only, they weren't there. The Union men who were there were standing tall and healthy, unharmed, surrendering their weapons and walking off with the strongbox with our men surrounding them.

A young lady approached me. "May I take your picture?" she asked as she held up her cell phone and aimed it's camera at me.

Steve had left the car. Outside, I saw Jake and the others leading away the prisoners. Badger followed behind. Steve was climbing down from the train.

I picked up my Enfield and hurried down the aisle while passengers returned to their seats. A teenager in a tee shirt snapped a picture as I passed him. The train's whistle blew. It would soon be on its way, and I didn't want to make this trip.

As I climbed down the steps, I turned before dropping to the ground, one hand holding the railing, the other holding my musket. I glanced back up into the car.

The Union officer with the drooping mustache stood at the top of the steps, blending with the shadows of the alcove. He was the man I had seen in the window before the train had stopped, the man whom the woman in the bonnet had denied seeing. He must have slipped past her and gone to the forward car. The straps on his shoulders signified him as a colonel. He smiled down at me, the expression giving me a chill rather than filling me with any warmth.

"See you on the field, soldier," he said.

I looked down as I dropped to the ground, and when I looked back up, he was gone.

Chapter Two

That day is a day of wrath, a day of trouble and distress, a day of wasteness and desolation, a day of darkness and gloominess, a day of clouds and thick darkness ... Zephaniah 1:15

The rolling hills of the Pine Creek Battlefield lay covered with the white peaks of canvas tents arranged in rows and formations, accented by larger command tents and flies, color added in the form of company and state flags rippling in the breeze. The smoke from dozens of cooking fires curled up into the noonday sky, carried away in the air. The aromas of various meals mingled in a savory collection. Just outside of the tiny Virginia town of Ramsey, the rock-strewn hills had been the site of a heated battle in August of 1864. Union troops had moved in and occupied the town. Confederate troops made a morning raid on their camp, sending the Federals running through the town to the other side, where they re-formed under their lieutenant general. They rallied and beat back the Confederates, who lost heavily upon this second battle. A few skirmishes followed, but the Confederates eventually went further south and the town stayed under Union occupation.

Sitting under the shade of our fly, on ground that had seen the footsteps and blood of soldiers of both blue and gray a hundred and fifty years ago, I absently stirred bits of chicken and noodles on my tin plate with my three-pronged fork. It was an antique fork, pitted with age, maybe not from the 1860's, but close to that era. I thought of those Confederate soldiers I had seen outside the train, men who had murdered unarmed Union soldiers. And then I had seen our own men and the men who were now enjoying lunch in the Union camp about a mile away on the other side of the battlefield park. Where had those first men come from, and where had they gone? The answer was obvious. They hadn't been there to begin with. What I had seen had looked so real, but no way could it have been. A man had been killed, shot in the head. That had not happened. No one had been shot like that in Ramsey for the past hundred and fifty years, and I had not seen ghosts. Ghosts don't appear in broad daylight to perform a little vignette for the entertainment of a single spectator. Besides, ghosts do not exist. The whole episode had been an hallucination, no doubt brought on by the heat. That, and stress. Maybe mostly stress.

Captain Jake Boden, our company commander, dropped down in the wooden camp chair beside me, a tin cup of steaming coffee cradled in both hands. He was a tall, rangy man, limbs long and lean from a lifetime of endless walking. His face was brown from the sun, lined and weathered, his salt-and-pepper hair cut short in a military style. He reminded people of a younger Clint Eastwood and gave the impression of a military officer. He fit his Confederate captain's uniform as well as it fit him, though he would look more natural with a horse under him. He even made his mail carrier's uniform look military issue. "Not hungry?" he asked.

I stared down at the cold mass congealing on my plate. "Whatever gave you that idea?" I asked.

He sipped his coffee. It must have burned his lips, since it came right from the pot on the grate over the campfire. Yet, he smacked his lips in delight. Why he drank such boiling hot liquid on such a steamy hot afternoon, I could not even guess. "Good raid today, Frank. The people seemed to like the show."

"It was quite a show," I admitted. My thoughts dwelt on the performance only I witnessed.

"You okay for the battle this afternoon?"

"Sure. Why not?" I didn't sound very enthusiastic.

He didn't bother looking at me, but looked out over the camp. "Well, I was talking to Steve. He said you were lookin' a bit pale earlier. You feel okay? Heat getting to you?"

"Jake, we're wearing wool, for goodness sake. It must be ninety out here. If the heat wasn't bothering me then I'd start to worry." What else could I say? That I was going insane? I was hallucinating, seeing things that just weren't there. Something had to be wrong with the old wiring, but I wasn't about to admit that. I wasn't about to mention what I saw, or thought I saw, not even to my son. Sure, I had just finished a rather strenuous year. A year filled with even more problems than the year before, a year that had ended very badly. That came with the territory. Teaching got harder each year, not easier, and there was always the possibility of really big problems, an unavoidable tragedy. Students were tougher, more difficult to deal with, harder to reach. And each day I had to come up with new ways to make science interesting to dozens of high school students who could not care less. Bring out the dancing science teacher. Juggle a few seashells, balance a frog on the end of my nose, unravel a double helix before their eyes.

And then there was that little incident two weeks before the end of the school year.

I was getting too old for that sort of thing, and retirement seemed a century away. It was time for a career change. I did it once, I could do it again. My letter of resignation was sitting on my desk at home, waiting for my decision to drop it in the mail. This was the beginning of August, but the board would have enough time to get a replacement, even if they had to use a substitute for the beginning of the school year.

What would I do next? My vague plan was to return to research, but that might be difficult after ten years. Maybe some other profession with less stress, something that wouldn't prompt hallucinations.

Jake seemed happy enough. Maybe the postal service wasn't as disagreeable as I was led to believe. I could become a letter carrier. Lots of fresh air and exercise, few people to deal with. Not a bad job. Jake had that edge of melancholy, though, something he shoved aside when he was out among the other reenactors. What lay just beneath the surface, creeping out to haunt his eyes now and then when he stared into the campfire or, like now, just off toward the horizon? He clutched his tin cup and gazed through the steam, lost to the activities around us. The expression that pulled his eyes reminded me of pain, but not physical. Was it the loneliness he felt at home, with no wife or family to share his life? I could only guess how that would feel to me, to have no family, to have emptiness. Or did his career carry its own form of stress that wore down on him?

His grin flashed, his eyes focusing on the camp around us, and the pain submerging once more. No, I wouldn't be able to handle the postal service. Endless walking a route or endless standing and sorting.

"We'll have a great day for a battle, Frank," he said. "Lots of spectators. If you don't feel good, take an early hit."

"Someone sick?" asked a gruff voice.

From out of the smoke of the campfire, Doc's short, round figure waddled toward us. He wiped his hands on a checkered towel. His suspenders hung down loose and his shirt sleeves were rolled up to his elbows, exposing an anchor tattooed on his forearm. His old sky-blue wool trousers and homespun cotton shirt were stained from all the meals he had prepared over the years of reenactment events. Born Terrance Carmine, he earned his nickname as a Navy medic during the latter days of the Vietnam War. Returning to civilian life, he had become a paramedic for a number of years, eventually retiring to the less stressful life of a short order cook at his own downtown diner. He wasn't a bad cook. The meals tended to be greasy, but at least they had flavor. Had I eaten the chicken and noodles earlier, they would have proved tasty. However, I wasn't in much of a mood for eating. Insanity seemed to ruin the appetite.

I could do a little cooking. What would a job in his diner be like? The pay would be terrible and the work hectic. I'd been through that, decades ago while working my way through college. No, if I did anything in the food service industry it would be more in the line of management, of which I knew nothing. I could train as an EMT, ride an ambulance and save lives. But I would also have to look death in the face. I couldn't do that again.

"Everything's fine, Doc," I told him, flashing him a half-hearted grin just to alleviate any misgivings.

He stared down at my tin plate and scowled. "Doesn't look like it to me. What's wrong, you don't like my cooking? Maybe you'd like something else, a barbecue or a cheeseburger."

"Thanks, Doc. Maybe later." I knew he wasn't serious, even without the sarcastic tone. He wasn't about to take a special order. Besides, he and Steve had already cleaned out the pots and pans. Everyone else had finished up their lunch and had cleaned up their own plates and utensils. I was the last one.

"Oh, so you don't like my cooking, then."

"Well, now that you mention it …" I lifted the plate and took a tentative sniff, then screwed my face in disgust.

"Well, maybe if you wouldn't play with it and let it get cold. Usually my customers can't wait to eat what I cook." He defiantly put his fists on his hips. Had he been in a three-piece suit he would have looked like a short, stocky, balding mobster contemplating putting a contract out on me.

"And it's good for them that their cook is also a paramedic," I pointed out. "Saves time. They don't have to wait for the ambulance."

Doc gave a rough approximation of a chuckle. "As if I hadn't heard that one before."

"First time today, I bet." I got up and walked over to the fire, then scraped the mutilated meal from my plate onto the burning logs under the iron grate. It hissed and smoked.

Doc followed me to the fire pit. "You don't look so good, Frank."

I began washing off my plate in the pot of soapy water. The water had been hot earlier, but had cooled by the time I came to it. It was cloudy and I tried to convince myself that the soap was the cause. I tugged a paper towel from my pocket and wiped away the remnants of greasy water. I dropped the damp towel onto the logs, where it sizzled and burst into flames.

"Is that your professional opinion, Doc?" I asked.

"Yep."

"I'm fine. Never better." Despite losing my mind, but then that had been coming ever since I started teaching. Okay, maybe before that. But dealing with high school students for ten years had taken its toll. I was just suffering some burn-out, though I should have improved with two months of summer vacation behind me, not getting worse. Maybe it was the stress from the realization that summer vacation was almost gone.

"Just make sure you keep drinking water during the day, not just during the battle," he said, the twist of his frown indicating he still didn't believe me. "Too many people make the mistake of drinking only on the battlefield. You've got to hydrate yourself. Unless you want to sit it out and keep me company."

Doc didn't participate in the battles anymore, not since his heart attack during Pickett's Charge in Gettysburg two years earlier. He stayed behind the lines, ready to lend a medical hand with a haversack loaded with equipment more modern than the nineteenth century, although we accused him of harboring leeches. His antique and replica instruments and paraphernalia stayed on display at his tent and were a favorite among the younger tourists who visited the camp between battles.

"I'll be fine. Steve will keep an eye on me."

Steve approached us, his kepi tipped back on his wavy blond hair. Like the rest of us, he was in his cotton shirt, a light-blue one wrinkled and now almost dry. Like the rest of us, his shirt had been soaked from time under his shell jacket. Both our jackets were draped over the peak of our tent, allowing the sun to dry the damp inner lining. The fresh breeze also helped the smell.

"Feeling okay, Dad?"

I groaned. "I wish people would stop asking me that. I'm fine."

"Good," he said so quickly that I wondered if he actually heard me. Teenagers tend to have selective hearing. I'd seen enough evidence of the syndrome over the last ten years. "Some of the guys are going over to the sutlers. Want to go?"

"Sounds like a plan," I said. At least it would stop me from moping around camp, dwelling in my own delusions.

I tossed my plate and utensils into our tent, then joined Steve, Badger, Charlie and Daniel. We trudged through the camp, then over a hill toward the edge of the battlefield. Near the entrance to the field, along the main road, stood the cluster of large tents used by the sutlers displaying their merchandise, from weapons and uniforms to books and art prints. Some specialized in women's period clothing; others in uniforms, at least one with only hats, and others with leathers and weapons. One man in a frock coat and tall hat took period-style photographs. He had plenty of clothing on hand for the civilian tourists to get into the act. There were food vendors and musicians. And crowds of people in tee shirts and jeans mingled with women in hoop dresses or long skirts, men in blue or gray, and men in period civilian suits. The crowds were thickening in anticipation for the afternoon battle and the opportunity to tour the Union and Confederate camps.

Badger, towering over me, pursed his lips beneath the shrubbery of his beard. "You—"

I stabbed my finger threateningly at him. "Don't even ask. I'm fine."

He grinned and his face, what was visible above his thick beard, brightened like that of a giant gnome. His blue eyes actually twinkled. "Cool."

I had no idea where he had gotten his nickname, and considering his imposing size, I never had the urge to ask. He had been a member of a notorious motorcycle gang and had led a rather disreputable life into his late thirties. He didn't like to talk about it and we never asked. What he did talk about was his new-found faith as a born-again believer and his passion for history, particularly the Civil War. He apparently did not exist beyond those two subjects and his motorcycle sales and repair business. He could not erase the tattoos and the scars, but he could smile as he did now, the gleam in his eyes showing off his new spirit and outshining any remnant of his dubious past. He's not a person you would want to upset, but then in the short time I had known him, he had never shown the slightest bit of anger. That was why I could tease him and not endanger my life. But I wouldn't push my luck.

He was content in his new life, and I wondered about work in a motorcycle shop. Considering that I had never been on a motorcycle; that was another career I was unqualified for.

Charlie, the only one of us who had changed into a clean shirt and a gray wool vest, looked less like a Civil War private than a stylish actor. His goatee was trimmed to perfection and his wavy hair was combed back just right. He walked as though he had just entered onto a stage and his performance had begun. He sold insurance, or at least that was the latest thing he sold. He was a born salesman. I wasn't. Sales never interested me and I doubt I could talk someone into buying a stick of gum—even if I paid for it.

He nudged an elbow into my ribs.

I followed a nod from his head toward two young women in shorts and tee shirts. Their shirts had different Civil War logos, but each carried a dominant Confederate battle flag.

I frowned at him. "What would Marie say?" I asked.

He grinned. "She's not here, Frank."

She never was. She refused to go to any of our events, even the ones close to home. Charlie never said why, never let on that there was any trouble between them, but he never let her absence get in the way of his enjoying the weekend. He was in his mid twenties and clinging hard to his youth. The young ladies noticed him noticing them, and they smiled back at him.

He nudged me again. "I'll catch up with you later, Frank."

"Don't ..." But he was already on his way to intercept the tourists. I wasn't sure whether I was going to warn him about missing our battle later or to admonish him for his intended behavior. Or both. He wouldn't have listened anyway.

Daniel had stopped in front of one sutler displaying new uniforms and watched Charlie wander off. He shook his head slowly, then went back to examining the gray shell jackets hanging on a rack. He was in his shirt and gray trousers, with his gray kepi perched on his shaved head. The white cotton shirt contrasted against his chocolate skin. He lifted his period-style wire-framed glasses to inspect one of the jackets.

One woman in a group passing near us stopped and stared at him. She was heavy set, dressed in tights and bulging out of a short tee shirt obviously too small for her. Her skin was a shade lighter than Daniel's and she eyed him with disgust. Two other women, who were less gaudily dressed, stopped with her, flanking her a step behind with embarrassed expressions on their faces.

"You should be ashamed of yourself!" she snapped. New Jersey spilled off her tongue. "What's up with this, dressed like a rebel? You their slave or somethin'? That's disgusting. We fought for our freedom, and here you is, on the side of the slaver. You oughta be ashamed."

Daniel set his glasses back in place and looked at her as though surprised she was addressing him.

"Madam," Daniel said in his deep, James Earl Jones voice, "I am afraid you are under a misconception. Actually, a number of misconceptions. First, the Civil War, War Between the States, or whatever euphemism you prefer, was not fought in order to free the slaves, it was fought over the rights of states versus the control of the federal government. If you had studied history instead of digesting rhetoric you would understand the political and economical ramifications."

"Oh, man," Badger said as he came up next to me. "Here we go again. We better grab him before he gets carried away."

Daniel babbled on in his best barrister's voice, as though he was delivering his closing statement in court for the defense of a falsely accused client. We'd heard his speech before, in various incarnations, not that it was memorized or even thought out. He was sensitive about the subject and became passionate and began spouting historical data and references.

"Also," he said, winding down, giving this woman an abbreviated version of his lecture, "at least one of my ancestors participated in the war on the side of the Confederate States and rose to the rank of corporal. He was not a slave, though his predecessors had come to this country as slaves, captured in Africa by other Africans, sold to Muslims who sold them to traders from New England, and brought here on ships built in Massachusetts."

The woman's mouth hung open. One of her friends smiled and batted her eyes at Daniel.

The woman shuffled one foot in front of the other and slowly stepped away from us. Badger and I flanked Daniel, but the event was over before we could lay our hands on his arms to lead him away.

I slapped Daniel's shoulder. "Come on. Someone's playing music up ahead. Let's check it out."

He shook his head, his features falling as though deflated. "Frank, I'm getting tired of the ignorance of people. And I'm getting tired of arguing my point of view every time someone sees me dressed in a Confederate uniform. Heck, I'm not even wearing my shell jacket. I'm treated as though I am some sort of traitor, even if they don't say anything."

What could I say? I could make a joke and laugh it off and be in danger of belittling his attitude. I couldn't come up with anything sage since I could not place myself in his position. We understood him, but he'd been with us for over two years.

"Well," I said, "you can't change everyone, and you can't make an impression overnight. You do your best."

"Yeah, but it's wearing me down. I'm tired of arguing."

"Daniel, you're a lawyer, that's in your job description."

"I haven't been in court for years," he said. "Besides, I didn't become a lawyer to argue, I did it to make a lot of money."

I shook my head sadly at him. "Haven't done that yet, have you?"

"In the middle of Pennsylvania? You've got to be kidding. Maybe I should go into politics."

"Now there's an idea. Move into a career with a better reputation than law." We drew closer to the music, a fiddler playing lively music. I said, "I'm thinking of a career change myself."

"You're going to leave the education profession?"

I nodded. "My resignation is addressed and stamped, lying on my desk at home, unless Sarah already dropped it in the mail. I'm going to send it as soon as we get home."

Daniel glanced over at me, suspicious. "You're kidding. What do you intend to do? Frank, you've been teaching for over eight years."

"Ten," I corrected.

"That long? Still, what do you intend to do? That's a long time to invest in a career and then just walk away. What about your pension, your retirement plan? Are you planning on going back into research?"

"That's the plan," I said. "I still know a few people in the industry. They like to use people with teaching backgrounds for pharmaceutical sales. Maybe I'll try for that."

Daniel shook his head. "You aren't a salesman, Frank."

"Thanks for the vote of confidence. Maybe I'll go back to school, get a law degree."

He wagged his finger in the air. "Now that is what our profession needs, one more lawyer."

"How about a paralegal?" I asked.

"Can you type?"

"With two fingers," I said, holding up the members and wiggling them. His frown was not encouraging.

Badger and Steve had moved just ahead of us and we quickly caught up with them. Badger stopped short and I halted beside him. Daniel and Steve continued on toward the spirited sounds of music.

"Oh, man," Badger said in more of a moan.

His face twisted in pain. His eyes, beneath his wrinkled brow, were focused on some point ahead of us, and I followed them to the crowd surging between the tents. Two figures caught my attention simply because they were so out of place. Both man and woman were in their mid to late forties—the man's steel-gray hair, touched with faded red, was tied in a ponytail that dangled down his back; the woman's gray-streaked black hair hung in a long braid. The man was beefy, once muscular, but now his belly sagged over his wide leather belt. The woman's narrow waist was exaggerated by hips widened by time. Her leather pants were so tight they could have been a second skin. Both wore black tee shirts underneath leather vests, the sleeves of the shirts cut off to reveal numerous tattoos. She had tattooed chains encircling each tightly muscled biceps. His arms, still retaining some of their bulk and strength, were completely illustrated with old blue ink with an occasional splash of washed-out red. Each arm was a collage of death and violence.

The woman stopped first as she glanced our way. She elbowed her companion in the ribs and nodded in our direction.

"Badger!" the man bellowed.

"Oh, man." Badger groaned. For a moment I thought he was going to turn and run back to camp. But he stood his ground as the two hurried up to him. The woman reached him first and threw her arms around him. She planted a heavy kiss on his beard, in the approximate position of his lips. His eyes went wide and his hands shot up as though to ward off an attack, but he was too late.

The woman's companion gave a deep laugh and slapped Badger on the back. He was shorter than Badger, but still an inch or so taller than me. As he laughed, I noticed his lower front teeth were missing. His nose had been broken more than once and not competently repaired.

The woman finally let Badger loose. She smiled, and I could see that she had more of her own teeth than her friend. Above her high cheekbones, her eyes were a pale blue. She must have been very attractive when she was younger, with a look that favored an American Indian heritage. Even now, despite the lines of a hard life creasing her face, she still had an attractive quality.

"Where have you been, Badger?" she said, her fingers lacing around one strap of his suspenders.

"Haven't seen you in years," the man said.

"Been a long time, Red," Badger said, his tone more formal than I'd ever heard it. "How you been, Jewel?"

"Missin' you," Jewel said, tugging on the suspender strap.

"Never thought we'd see you again, man," Red said. "Thought you was dead or somethin'. What you doing here, dressed like that? You playing Civil War?"

"I'm a reenactor, Red."

"Right, man. You was always into that history stuff, weren't you?"

Jewel eyed Badger up and down. Her look reminded me of a hungry predator.

"That outfit don't look as comfortable as leather, Badger" she said. "You really dress up in those wool jackets and stuff?"

"Sure do," Badger said. "Hey, this is my friend, Frank. Frank, this is Big Red and Jewel, a couple of old friends."

"Nice to meet you," I said. I refrained from extending my hand, which would have been a wasted effort. Red and Jewel both glanced at me, Red gave a nod to acknowledge my existence, then they promptly returned to ignoring me. I felt invisible, but for once I didn't mind it.

"Been years, man," Red said, grinning wide with his missing teeth. "Haven't seen you since we was in Georgia. 'Member that? We really raised hell then, didn't we? That one sheriff would have put us away for twenty easy if he'd had caught us. Ain't seen you since. Really thought you was dead, since you never got in touch. Heard some rumors, though. One was that you was in the pen. You do time, Badger?"

"Nope." He kept glancing at me, as if searching for an exit, or as a drowning man looking for a life preserver. But what was I going to do? I wasn't about to drag him out of Jewel's clutches. Maybe if I had my musket or at least my bayonet, but not without some sort of weapon, and preferably with reinforcements.

"Hey, Badger," Jewel said as she tugged on both of his suspenders. "Why don't we all go to that place at the end of town, what's it called? Harley's?"

"Yeah," Red said, slapping his beefy hands together. "Let's grab a couple beers and catch up on things. Bet you're hot in that stuff. It's a scorcher of a day, man."

Badger shook his head. "Nah. I don't drink any more."

"And Red don't drink any less!" Jewel doubled over in laughter at her own joke. Red joined in.

Then Red sobered and shook his finger toward Badger. "Hey, man. I heard you gone religious or somethin' like that. That it?"

Badger shrugged. "Something like that." He was usually a bit more forthcoming about his faith, taking any opportunity to talk about it among the other reenactors. I wondered why he seemed so reluctant to bring it up now.

"Haven't joined one of those communes, have you?"

"Nah!" Jewel said with a slap against Red's arm. "He wouldn't be here playing Johnny Reb if he was in one of those. Come on with us anyway, Badger. One beer won't hurt none."

"Nope. But you can hang out and watch our battle later. It's really something. Pretty realistic. Maybe we can get together afterwards in our camp, and you can meet the other guys."

Jewel untangled herself from him and frowned. Her glare became icy. She apparently did not take rejection well.

Red shrugged. "Suit yourself. Maybe we'll stick around. Never liked this history stuff much, but my old man had some ancestor what was some rebel officer or something. Thought I'd look into my roots."

Jewel poked her finger into Badger's chest. "We'll hang around, Badger. You ain't gettin' away so easy. You ran out once. I ain't lettin' you do that again."

"Later, man," Red said as he put his arm over Jewel's shoulder. They walked off together.

I caught sight of Steve and Daniel, and Badger and I began moving to catch up with them. Badger's chin bounced on his chest. He stayed quiet, his eyes watching the ground just in front of his feet. From up ahead came the strains of a fiddler playing a wild jig.

"Nice couple," I said. I tried not to put any sarcasm in my words, but some leaked out.

Badger grunted.

"Old friends?" I said.

This time he snorted. "We rode together, long time ago," he said. He never went into details about that era, and I doubt any of us knew the name of the gang he rode with, let alone the sort of trouble they caused. "Thought that part of my life was long gone. Man, what's the odds of them showing up?"

"Some things we just can't control," I said, thinking again of my own impending insanity. "Seems like you guys were pretty close. Especially you and Jem."

"Jewel," he corrected, missing the fact that I knew the name and had mispronounced it on purpose. "Yeah, well, that was a long time ago. I ain't the same person they used to know. I ain't the same Badger."

I wondered what his real name was and why he never used it. What kind of name would make the nickname Badger sound better? "They don't seem to realize that," I said.

"Nope, and I should have told 'em." He frowned, but not at me, maybe at himself, maybe at the world in general. He fell into his own thoughts and stayed quiet until we came up to Steve and Daniel.

The music came from a young woman bending into a fiddle and sliding the bow back and forth over the strings so fast that it blurred. As she tossed her head, her long blond hair went flying in all directions. She was

"Old friends?" I said.

dressed in a period blouse and skirt of blue and the shoe of her right foot peeked out from the hem of the skirt and tapped rapidly to the beat. She was entirely absorbed in playing the instrument, oblivious of the crowd that had formed around her. A number of spectators clapped their hands and stomped their feet along with the music. Someone gave a loud whistle.

Steve, standing beside Daniel, was not one of the more energetic in the audience. He watched the girl intently, a stupid, lopsided grin on his face. Under the perspiration and tangled hair, she was pretty and about his age.

"Oh boy," I said.

"Huh?" he said, without taking his eyes from the musician.

Badger nudged me with his elbow. "He's got it bad."

"Yep," I said. I knew it would happen sooner or later.

I had never seen him like this, but then the young musician was impressive. She flashed a smile at the crowd, her blue eyes twinkling with excitement. Her hands blurred over the fiddle as she spun her tune. Then she brought the song to an abrupt end and stood panting, holding the bow away from the fiddle as though it would leap to the strings and begin the tune once more on its own. The crowd thundered its applause. Steve and I joined in, and the girl bowed low, her hair falling over her face. When she straightened, her cheeks were flushed and her eyes flitted away from the audience. She seemed embarrassed at the attention.

Daniel bent toward Steve and said, "So, go say hello. Introduce yourself."

Steve's face reddened. He shook his head. "Nah." He turned as if to leave.

Badger grunted and mumbled, "Kids."

Badger pushed his way through the crowd as it began to disperse. He walked up to the girl, towering over her like a skyscraper next to a small house. I couldn't hear what he said, but she smiled and nodded her head a few times.

No sense in letting Steve suffer humiliation. I turned with him to leave. "Come on, son. Let's have a look at some of the sutlers."

But Badger had other plans. He called out Steve's name and waved his hand emphatically. Steve shook his head, but Badger became more insistent. Reluctantly, Steve took a few hesitant steps to approach the young musician. His face was red and I could almost hear the burning thoughts of getting revenge on Badger at some later date. I decided to have a talk with Badger myself.

"Steve Blaine, Jenna Connor," Badger said. "Jenna, Steve. Jenna's a history buff, too, Steve. Thought you two might have a few things in common."

Badger instantly withdrew, giving Steve a small shove as he did so.

"Hi," Steve said in a weak voice. "I'm Steve."

"Yeah, I know." She laughed, but not in a way to ridicule. It was light, friendly, as musical as her playing. Steve laughed along.

"You play great," he said.

"Thanks. What unit are you with?"

"Thirteenth Virginia."

Badger gave me a wink as he passed me. "Give 'em some time. Let's take a walk."

I hesitated. Steve and his new friend were in the midst of a friendly conversation, which seemed to involve their respective schools, hometowns, and families. They looked like a couple of old friends, comfortable with each other. He had been distracted lately, preoccupied first with his graduation and now with his impending start as a freshman in college. Maybe some time with someone his own age would take his mind off that and let him relax. He'd eventually make his way back to camp before the battle. He might not get to visit any sutlers this morning, but I doubt if he'd care. I wondered if they'd ever get around to discussing history.

I turned to follow Badger and nearly bumped into a young woman.

She was dressed in period clothes, a frilly white blouse and a colorful long skirt. Her jewelry was overdone, with silver bracelets jangling on her wrists and necklaces dangling around her neck. Long silver earrings peeked out from behind waves of long black hair. Her bright brown eyes looked up at me and the corners of her lips curved in a wry smile. Her expression was easy and friendly and made me feel that I must know her from somewhere. She must have been in her early thirties and she was attractive enough for me to remember had we met before, but I couldn't place her.

"I'm sorry," I said after our collision.

"They make a nice couple," she said. I stared at her in confusion until she tilted her head toward Steve and his new friend. "They look nice together. Natural."

Her voice carried the light Virginia accent.

I turned and glanced at Steve, then back at the woman. "Yes they do. That's my son, Steve."

"I see the resemblance. I'm Jenna's mother."

I had to recalculate my estimation of her age, then decided she must have been a child bride. I saw no resemblance between her and her daughter, but refrained from saying so. She was dark, olive-skinned, with a Mediterranean look, while her daughter was fair. I held out my hand. "Frank Blaine."

"Miranda Connor," she said, taking my hand. Her skin felt cool despite the heat of the day, and when we touched, she shuddered as though I had given her an electric shock. Her eyes widened. "Oh. You are the one. I thought you might be."

"The one what?" I glanced around for a polite exit from a conversation that was on the verge of weird. I had lost sight of Badger and Daniel in the growing crowd.

"The one," she said as though that were explanation enough. "I can't say any more than that. You'll find out soon enough."

"Okay," I said. "It was nice meeting you. I'm just going to find my friends who have wandered off." Apparently insanity was not being selective this weekend. I wondered if this woman had been experiencing hallucinations.

She turned with me in a swirl of colorful skirt and wrapped herself around my arm in a movement too fast for me to notice until we were walking side by side. My face was burning and the perspiration ran more than from the heat. I wanted to extract myself, but I also didn't want to offend her. She was just overly friendly. Southern hospitality, that was it. She wasn't really flirting.

"You can't leave yet, Frank. Let our children get to know each other, and you can visit my tent."

"Your ... tent?" I began to pry myself free.

She laughed, tossing her hair and rattling her jewelry. She waved her hand toward the sutler's tent in front of us. Sure enough, a banner hung over the entrance proclaiming Connor's Curiosities. I tried to smile at her, but I felt stupid. I would have preferred to go back to camp and hide in my own tent until the battle, but she took my arm again and tugged me through the entrance. Inside were tables and displays, and half a dozen potential customers browsing. Once my eyes grew accustomed to the darker interior I saw framed artwork hung from tent posts and books arranged on tables.

"I usually come to a couple of these events each year," she said. "I have a shop in town, so it's nice when this event happens. I have someone running my shop while I'm here. I like to dress up, and Jenna loves history. She looks forward to this each year. Isn't she great on the fiddle? Picked it up when she was five and hasn't put it down since. I don't know who she takes after. I can't play a thing, and her father, well, he's a lawyer so you can tell how musical he is. Her talent could be from his side, though. That's the

Irish in her. She loves to play those jigs, and they go over so well at these events. Must have skipped a generation, since her father definitely isn't musical. He couldn't carry a tune in his briefcase."

"Your husband's a lawyer?" I managed to work in. I began browsing the artwork, framed prints by Kunstler, Troiani, Gallon, and others that I recognized. And then some rather odd works by artists I didn't know. These were bleak, ethereal works, some showing graveyards and grieving widows in Elizabethan black shrouds. Occasional works represented vague, vaporous figures of the dear departed still wearing their uniforms and carrying their muskets or sabers.

"My ex," she said, "he lives in Pennsylvania."

"So do we. My wife and I," I quickly pointed out. "Sarah. And our kids."

"Oh? She didn't come with you?"

"No," I said, reluctant to tell the truth. I moved away from her and looked over the rows of books laid out on the table. Most of the titles bore either the word ghost or spirit. Spirits of Gettysburg, Ghosts of the Old South, Civil War Haunts. I was beginning to see a trend.

"Unusual collection," I pointed out.

"Some very popular titles. This one mentions a few of the local hauntings, though not all of them. I've been thinking of writing my own book. Ramsey is quite an active community, there's so many places around here that are just bursting with energy. You can hardly walk three feet on this battlefield without feeling a spiritual essence. I conduct a tour in town, by the way. We visit places that have been known for visitations at some point in the past. Most of them concern the War Between the States, which is only natural since there were so many violent deaths here during that time, but some are from different eras. It's all very exciting. You and your son should come into town and join our tour. My treat."

"That's nice of you, but I don't—"

"I insist. You'll have fun. And," she gave that half smile again, as though she knew something I was not quite bright enough to figure out, "I have a feeling things might be very entertaining."

"We probably won't have the time, but I'll mention it to Steve." I had no intention of going, but I might go ahead and mention the tour to Steve. Maybe it would make him think twice about a friendship with Jenna. I edged closer to the tent's opening.

"I also do readings, if you're interested. It helps with my gypsy impression." She waved her hand toward a table, her bracelets jangling. On the table lay a deck of cards spread out, a number of them face up. I recognized a couple of the cards—the hangman, the lovers, others I had no names for. A typical tarot set, but with a very antiquated look. I wondered if they were antiques or replicas.

The exit seemed so far away.

"I don't think so," I said.

"No crystal ball, just the cards. But I am fairly accurate." She bent over the table and scooped all the cards into a pile, then began shuffling them. "What company are you in?"

"Company?" My mouth hung open for a moment while my brain tried to absorb her question. I was about to explain that I was a teacher and didn't work for a company. Then I realized she was asking about our reenactment group. I told her which unit we belonged to.

She stopped shuffling. "Isn't that the one established locally?"

"Yes, a local militia, men from Ramsey and the surrounding area."

Cards held in one hand, she wrapped her arms around herself in a jingle of jewelry and tapped a polished nail against her pursed lips. "Hmm. I remember now. Your company has a rather infamous history. It was one of the companies mustered not long after the start of the war. Most were farmers, but a few were merchants and clerks from Ramsey. You know about the train incident."

For a moment I didn't think about escaping. I stared at her while a cold memory flashed through my mind. A man standing outside the train, firing a Minié ball into the brain of an unarmed soldier. I didn't want her to continue. I knew what she was going to say and it was even more disturbing than the hallucination I had experienced.

"The Confederates would raid the trains," she said, "which were still controlled by the North. General Jackson was quite ingenious in his dealings with the trains passing through Harper's Ferry. Around Ramsey, our men would occasionally stop the trains and confiscate anything worthwhile. Your men stopped one up north and took the cash box slated to pay Union troops in the west. Witnesses said the Union soldiers surrendered but were killed anyway. The cash box disappeared. It was never turned over to the Confederate command, and the officers of the company claimed there was no box. I believe there was an investigation, charges were brought by the railroad company, but no trial came of it. Not enough evidence, I guess. After the war, none of the men of that company were left to answer the charges."

"None of them were left?" I echoed.

"No. I would have thought you would know that. Every one from that company was killed in the war. I can't remember the details, but that's pretty well-known around here since they were local boys. A tragedy. But it is an opportunity for some exciting visitations for Ramsey. We're a small town, but to have so many violent losses around here and involving native sons, well, it just opens so many supernatural doors. For instance, at Pennyworth's Farm, homestead of one of those soldiers from your company, a man in gray appears wandering around the outside of the barn, as though searching for a way in. It's exciting."

For her and her business, maybe. But it was not very comforting to know that we were reenacting a group accused of war crimes and who all died before the end of the war. Even less comforting was the reality that lay behind the hallucination I had experienced on the train. How can I hallucinate some historical event I never knew had occurred?

Chapter Three

The people which sat in darkness saw great light; and to them which sat in the region and shadow of death light is sprung up ... Matthew 4:16

"Shoulder ... Arms!"

We squeezed together in two rows, our ranks stretching out over the crest of the hill, our shoulders rubbing. Left hands reached over to lift muskets, right hands gripping the weapons at the base of the stock, fingers wrapping around the trigger guard. We had marched from the camp half a mile away, stopped to bake in the hot afternoon sun, then marched a little further. The Union camp was visible at the far end of the battlefield, tops of canvas tents glaring white. Between us and those tents stood ranks of blue uniforms. To the left of them, cannon coughed puffs of smoke, then bellowed their volley. Behind us, at the edge of our own camp, Confederate cannon roared to reply. The ground vibrated.

"Battalion ..." called out our commander, Colonel Wessner.

"Company ..." echoed the various company captains.

"Forward ... March!"

Down the slope we went, each of us trying to watch our footing and the line of men on either side of us. I grabbed hold of the edge of the sleeve of Charlie's shell jacket on my left to help us keep in line. On my right, Steve took hold of my sleeve. Behind me, I felt Daniel touch my belt to keep the proper distance between front and rear ranks. We jostled and bumped into each other as we marched, but our ranks held their form.

To our right were the distant bleachers and crowds of spectators. From our angle they were soon lost to us. Without them or the parking area or the highway in sight and the cannon masking the noise of traffic, and with the smoke of cannon fire rolling over the hills, we became lost to the past. We marched across the fields and a hundred and fifty years slipped away.

"It is quite hot, Captain," Sam said.

Jake Boden stifled a smile. He held his saber up and kept pace with our company. "Watch your step, boys."

Rocks and weeds slipped underfoot. Our brogans gave us little traction. I tried to concentrate on my steps, keeping pace with my fellow soldiers, and think of the impending battle. However, my mind kept gravitating toward Miranda Connor's dissertation on the history of our company. I had tried to corner Jake about her accusations, but there had been no time. I remembered something about the company's history and the original roster on the company's Web site Jake maintained, but I had never read it. I may have glanced over it, but I could not recall anything so depressing as accusations of murder and theft, or that none of the original members of the company had survived to the end of the war. I could not say it wasn't there—I just believed I would have remembered something so drastic. Of course, this provided a good explanation for my hallucination paralleling Ms. Connor's words. I had no doubt suffered from the heat, and in such a state I hallucinated about something I had indeed read but couldn't consciously remember. My subconscious memory took control and created a vision of that atrocity. It was a simple enough explanation, one that lifted my spirits. It didn't quite explain the odd fellow in the blue uniform and the drooping mustache, but I put him in with the hallucination just because he had been so strange. Heat does some unusual things to people. Hallucinations are not so far-fetched. Even I am not immune.

Union troops appeared on the crest of the foremost hill ahead of us. The first rank dropped to one knee. All muskets were raised, and a volley roared in unison. A billowing white cloud obliterated the blue troops.

"Battalion ... Halt! Load and to the ready!"

I swung my musket in front of me, reached around and dug my hand into my cartridge box. I took the paper cartridge, tore the top away, and poured the black powder into the musket's muzzle. I tapped the rifle on the ground to settle the powder, lifted it to tuck the stock under my right arm, then cocked the hammer. I took a cap from the pouch and thumbed it onto the musket's nipple. I held the weapon ready. Up and down the ranks, over five hundred muskets were loaded and held ready.

"Aim!"

Muskets snapped up, hammers cocked full.

"Fire!"

The word was lost in the thunder of the volley.

As the smoke cleared, the Union troops were in retreat, pulling back from the crest of the hill. Half a dozen bodies littered the ground, sprawled in the grass. One man propped himself up on an elbow to watch the ensuing battle while the others lay as though dead. Our own lines bore spaces where men had dropped from the first strike.

"Load and to the shoulder!" came the command.

We reloaded quickly and cradled our muskets in our right hands once more. Then came the command to raise them to right shoulder shift and to march on the double. We ran up the hill, our ranks losing integrity, men scattered over the slope. At the top, we drew back into cohesive lines. The call came to form up on the colors, and we aligned our ranks to the flag bearers.

As we formed up, I looked down at a Union soldier sprawled at my feet. Blood covered his forehead and right temple.

"Hey, Yank," I said, tapping his foot with the toe of my brogan. "You okay?"

He lifted his head and one eye squinted against the sunlight. "Yeah, man. No problem." He laid back and resumed his imitation of death, mouth agape.

We marched forward, careful not to tread on any of the bodies of our enemy. On the next hill, the Union troops reformed their ranks. There seemed to be more of them, reinforcements taking up positions. The first two ranks started forward, rifles at shoulder arms, steps steady even on the downward slope. Behind them, the remaining ranks took their time in forming up, tightening their ranks and readying themselves for the next attack.

Our ranks faced the enemy in the shallow basin between the two hills. Wisps of smoke curled over the ground, clinging to the grass. Clouds must have blown over the sun, for the sky became overcast. I wondered if it might rain later. A cool breeze blew over the hill, chilling my skin. I shivered beneath my damp clothes.

The rows of Union soldiers came on, their faces shadowed under the brims of their kepis. Our own footsteps over the ground and the rattle of our accouterments masked the sounds of their approach. When would they stop and bring their weapons to bear?

When were we going to halt?

We drew closer, and I felt a surge of fear that real soldiers may have experienced on this field. How many had died on this very ground?

"Ah," I said to Steve, "don't you think we should be ready to shoot?"

"Huh?" he said without a glance at me. Sweat rolled down his nose to form a drop at the tip.

I looked over to Captain Jake. He didn't seem concerned about the approaching troops. His saber pointed upward and his eyes went from us to the ranks on top of the hill.

I expected to hear Colonel Wessner's command at any moment.

They were fifty yards away, and still we hadn't stopped. Forty yards. I could see their dirty faces and stained uniforms. Their faces bore the black powder stains from tearing the cartridge papers with their teeth. Their eyes, shadowed under their kepis, looked hollow. Cold, determined expressions.

Too close to fire, even with our blanks.

Did they intend to battle in hand-to-hand combat?

Ten yards.

They were on us, and still we were moving into them. How ridiculous was this maneuver? I don't pretend to be a historian, let alone an expert on military maneuvers. I was a scientist, a biology teacher. But still this made no sense.

The Union soldiers were on us, and I stopped dead.

Behind me, Daniel pushed me forward. I plunged into the foremost soldier, and a cold wind engulfed me.

I stopped again and looked around me. My own troops moved on, Steve craning his neck to look back at me, Badger and Daniel in the rear rank marching around me. Someone swore at me.

"Blaine!" I heard Jake Boden calling. "Get back in line!"

But I stood at the bottom of the hill, turning to watch the Union ranks marching silently up the slope we had just descended. The overcast sky began to clear, and the sunlight blazed through and bathed the hillside. As the light stretched across the hill, the ranks of blue troops dissolved in the glare. In a moment the hillside was bare.

Then Colonel Wessner himself ran over to me.

"Private," he said, his brows knitted with concern under his own kepi. "Are you okay?"

Behind me now, muskets exploded as our ranks met the Union's ranks on the hilltop. I glanced over my shoulder to see the battle rage. The Unions withdrew further, allowing our men to crest the hill. Then our men began pulling back, leaving wounded upon the hilltop.

When I looked back at the colonel, his eyes widened. "You're as white as a sheet, man. Get a drink and sit down before you drop over."

He gripped my arm, offering support.

I cradled my musket against my right arm and took my canteen. The water was still cool, and I must have drunk half of its contents.

"You okay?" he asked again.

"No," I said. "No, I'm not."

He told me to sit down and mumbled something about heat stroke. I was inclined to agree with him and I wasn't about to describe what I had just seen or why I had suddenly stopped. Heat was a good reason for my hallucinations. Either that or I was cracking up. I'd prefer the first explanation, but how many times can heat cause these hallucinations? Heat might cause a problem with a person's vision, but I doubted it could create such elaborate visions.

I dropped down on the hillside, vacantly aware of the raging battle. Wessner had moved on to shout orders.

Another figure appeared next to me, this one short and stocky, with a bloodstained apron tied around his bulging middle. Doc Carmine was in his impression of a field surgeon, wandering over the battlefield to tend the wounded. His big haversack hanging over his left hip contained modern emergency paraphernalia just in case some wound had actually occurred, as it sometimes did. And then there was the occasional heat stroke and heart attack. He also carried a canvas bucket, which he shoved at me. The ice inside rattled and sent a whiff of coolness across my face. I slipped off my kepi, took a handful of ice, dumped it into the kepi, then placed the cap back on top of my head. My hair was already soaked with sweat. It took some time before I could feel any trace of coldness. I popped a couple chunks of ice into my mouth.

"Doc," I said, mumbling around the ice. Cold water dribbled down my chin. "I'm cracking up."

He dropped down beside me with a grunt, his knees cracking with the effort. When he was settled, he patted my knee. "Happens to the best of us, kid."

We watched the battle rage over the hill. Cannon boomed on either side. Muskets thundered. Wisps of smoke rolled over the ground like early morning fog. Our lines broke upon a retreat, and our officers rallied the remaining men for one more charge. The Union ranks held, and our brave Confederates fell under volley after volley. The survivors pulled back and the bugle sounded to bring an amiable end to the conflict. We had inflicted our own share of casualties upon the Union side, but they were clearly the winners. This time.

Exhausted and hot soldiers limped by. The dead and wounded scattered over the hills arose and headed toward their respective camps. They shuffled along, in no hurry, catching up with comrades, chatting about the event.

Badger huffed up. A red-stained muslin rag was tied around his head, pulled down over his right ear and giving the impression that the appendage had been shot off. One hand clutched his battered old slouch hat. He dropped his musket next to mine, then plopped down beside me. His big hand dug into Doc's canvas bucket and came out dripping. He popped ice into his mouth one at a time and crunched on them as though he was eating popcorn. He never said a word, but watched the men stagger by. We could have been in a theater watching a 3-D movie.

Captain Jake came next, with his sword in its scabbard cradled over one shoulder. He sat down next to Doc and began balancing the saber in the air by its hilt.

Steve dropped next to Badger, laid back and pushed his kepi down over his eyes. Badger passed the bucket toward him. One hand searched blindly for the ice, found some, and shoved pieces into his mouth.

"Are we all here, now?" I said. "Should we wait for the rest of the company?"

Daniel came by, followed soon by Sam and Charlie. Sam sat down in the grass while the other two stood, leaning on their muskets. Sam pulled off his hat and wiped away sweat with the back of his hand.

"Frank's cracking up," Doc said.

"Is that your professional medical opinion?" Jake asked, still concentrating on balancing his sword.

"Nope. It's his. My professional opinion is that it's almost supper time."

I frowned at Doc. "Whatever happened to doctor/patient confidentiality?"

"I'm not a real doctor," Doc said with a shrug. "I just play one on television."

"So," Badger said between chomps of ice, "what makes you think you're crackin' up?"

These were my friends, right? I could confide in them. Right?

I took a moment to try to gather the right words, then decided there was no way I could make this sound reasonable. Searching for the best way to relate what happened, I realized that it was indeed crazy. "We marched right through a line of Union soldiers," I said. It sounded worse than it actually had been. Maybe I should have just ignored the whole incident. Trouble was, it wasn't my first experience.

No one spoke.

I looked at each of them. Steve looked like he was asleep, hat still covering his face, hands clasped to make a pillow under his head. Jake brushed some dirt from his dented brass scabbard. Doc dug into his haversack for something. Badger just watched the men clearing the field and tossed another chunk of ice into his mouth. Daniel dug a handkerchief from his pocket, slipped off his glasses, and began polishing the lenses. Charlie straightened his belt and brushed dirt from the front of his shell jacket. Sam poured water from his canteen over his thinning hair. Maybe they thought I was joking, or maybe they were affirming with their silence that I was indeed going insane.

"You don't say," Badger said after a while.

Jake leaned forward to look at me from around Doc. "I take it you don't mean those guys up on the hill. Was this when you stepped out of rank?"

Daniel pointed his glasses at me and squinted to bring me into focus. "I was wondering what happened. My advice is to admit nothing. Nobody buys an insanity plea anymore."

"That's when it happened," I said, ignoring Daniel's advice against my own better judgment. "They were marching down in front of the others, and I was wondering why no one was ordering us to fire on them, or why they didn't shoot at us. Then we were right on top of them. I thought we were going to collide, but then they were behind us. We walked right through them."

Jake was nodding. "And you're not kidding about this, are you?"

"Dad doesn't kid about stuff like that," Steve said. He wasn't asleep after all, but he never bothered to lift his kepi.

I tossed up my hands. "I guess this sort of thing may happen to you guys all the time, but it's the first time I've hallucinated on this scale."

"So you think it was a hallucination?" Doc asked.

"Well it wasn't real," I said. I frowned at him, annoyed.

"Maybe it was the ghost regiment," Jake said.

"There are no ghosts!" I snapped. "I was just seeing things."

"Doin' drugs?" Badger asked. "Used to see some weird stuff myself, back in the eighties."

I was about to admit that I had seen some strange things in the eighties too—none of which had to do with drugs, legal or otherwise—but I decided to ignore Badger's reference. "It's just the heat."

"Could be," Doc said. "We'd better get you out of the sun, get plenty of fluids into you. I'll check you over back at camp. But you don't look like you're suffering from heat stroke. Maybe exhaustion."

"I think he's just burnt out," Steve said. "It happens after teaching too many years. Especially in high school."

"Thanks for your vote of confidence," I told my son.

Jake climbed to his feet, using the saber to prop himself up. "I still think it's the ghost regiment. This is the actual battlefield, you know. A lot of men died on this very spot." He jabbed the scabbard down for emphasis.

"I thought ghosts wait until midnight," I said, getting to my own feet. "This is afternoon. Are their internal clocks screwed up? Can't they tell day from night? Besides, I was the only one who saw them."

"Are you sure about that?" Jake asked.

I lifted up my hands to point out the obvious. "You didn't notice any other idiots falling out of rank because they thought they were going to run right into an enemy army? Anyone else go into shock?"

"No," Doc said, "but there were a couple who had succumbed to heat exhaustion. The paramedics were busy today. You aren't that pale and you aren't clammy, so I don't think a trip to the emergency room is called for. The heat still probably affected you, though. I suggest you take it easy, get plenty of fluids, and stay away from seances."

Recalling Miranda and her stack of tarot cards, I promised, "Definitely."

Doc caught my arm to stop me while the others went on toward camp. He waited until the last was out of earshot, then he leaned toward me and whispered, "Frank, you're under a lot of stress. The heat's bad enough, but what you went through two months ago is enough to drive anyone over the edge."

I stopped short and stared at him. I hadn't been aware he knew about it. Maybe they all knew. Maybe Jake was just trying to help with his nonsense about a ghost regiment. Well, of course they all knew what happened. It had been in all the news reports for days and on the front page in the papers as far away as Pittsburgh. But my involvement wasn't public knowledge. I hadn't talked about it, so I assumed no one else knew I had been there.

"It takes time to get over something like that," he said.

"I just happened to be there when it happened."

"It was more complicated than that, from what I heard," he said, tipping his head to eye me knowingly.

I wasn't about to relive it. The dreams were bad enough.

"Look, Frank, I just want you to know you can talk with me if you need to. Not everyone's been through something like that."

"Now you're a psychologist?" I said in a lame attempt to lighten the dialogue.

"Nah. Just thinking of becoming a bartender and wanted to get in some practice counseling the customers."

But he didn't smile. Of any of the guys, Doc would understand. He had seen people die, some who had been his friends. He had seen action in Vietnam during two tours of duty, and he had been a paramedic for a number of years. True, it was in a small city, but tragedies still happened. What he suggested made sense. It helped explain my voyage toward insanity. Somehow, it still didn't comfort me.

"Thanks, I'll keep it in mind," I said, then started up the hill.

*****

I cornered Jake Boden later, under the shade of the camp fly. Most of the others had wondered off, either to the sutlers or to other encampments. Doc was at his own tent, where his display of period medical paraphernalia captured the interest of the younger members of families touring the camp. Dressed in his red-stained apron, Doc set about explaining the tools and medical procedures of the time.

"Jake," I said, "you know the history of our company, right?"

"Sure. It's on the Web page. Haven't you read it? Came right out of the book on company histories."

I didn't want to admit that I hadn't read the Web page, strictly speaking. Skimming part of it might qualify, so I nodded. "Yeah, but I heard something that I don't remember reading." Which was entirely true. "It was about members of the company robbing a train and keeping what was taken."

Jake pursed his lips and stared at the dirt, knocking a few pebbles with the toe of his boot. He stayed quiet for a long time, and I got the impression he was waiting for me to grow bored and leave. I didn't, and he realized he had to answer.

"Yep. Some of the local boys. The company was made up of men from Ramsey and some of the surrounding farms. Started out as a militia, then became part of the Army of Northern Virginia. There were some rumors, but I don't think it was ever in the papers, and no one was brought to trial. I saw some letters of the period owned by local families who are descendants of the original soldiers. They made references to the train raids. They happened a lot back then. But this one time I think you mean was different. Instead of just robbing the train, the raiders killed all the Union soldiers, and maybe after the Federals were disarmed. That's one of the sore points. If they were disarmed, then killed, that's obviously murder and considered a war crime. To make matters worse, the contents of the strongbox, either gold or Federal dollars, was never passed along to the right Confederate officials. Still, I never found anything official. No one was charged, though some of the local families blamed Captain Howard Long, company commander. Him and a couple of other men from the company who had less-than-stellar backgrounds. By the end of the war, they were dead, so nothing could be learned. The event just seemed to fade into obscurity."

"Did any of the members of the company survive the war?" I asked.

"Ah, no. I thought I put that in the company's history on the Web." His tone suggested that he had deliberately left out that little tidbit of historical information.

"Maybe," I said, giving him the benefit of the doubt. After all, I hadn't read everything. "What ever possessed you to reenact a group where everyone died?"

He shrugged. "Seemed a good idea at the time. I like Ramsey—it's a nice little town. Maybe I should have done more research before I registered it. Anyway, we haven't had any problems for the past five years, and no fatalities."

"Not yet," I pointed out, then had a sudden regret over my attempt at humor.

"If I had known about Captain Long…" He let his words drop away. I waited, but he had fallen to stare at the dirt again.

"What about Long? Do you mean that train raid?"

His face sagged. "Yep. Long seemed to have a great reputation, a good, honest man, a good leader. I've seen letters that spoke highly of his integrity and field reports from superior officers that described his bravery and ingenuity. After all, he was just a farmer and had been made company commander over some men who had political ties. But that one incident put a dark cloud over his career and the company in general. Nasty rumors followed them, and … well, they all were killed off eventually. That's a great situation to start rumors about a curse. There's even local stories about the men haunting their homes, like the one man who is seen wandering around his farm, as though searching for a way in but never finding it. The curse of Ramsey's Raiders. Serves me right for not doing my research. It figures, the way my luck goes. Story of my life."

"More than just that company were wiped out," I said, though that was a strange way to try to cheer somebody up.

"Yeah." His voice lowered, as though he really didn't want to say more.

For some time neither of us talked. We watched some tourists walk past, nodding to them in greeting. Another group came to visit Doc, and he went into his lively dissertation. Then Jake turned toward me. "How did you find out about the train incident? That isn't on our Web site, and not everyone knows about it. Most people around here aren't thrilled to advertise what their local boys did."

"A local." I searched for the best words to describe Miranda Connor. I found many good words, but all too elaborate and inappropriate. "She told me about it when she found out what company we were in."

His eyes brightened. "Not that young girl Steve was talking about?"

"No. Her mother." Word does travel fast in camp.

Jake wrinkled his brow and searched inwardly.

"Miranda Connor," I said, saving him from wandering through his memory.

He rolled his eyes at obvious recognition of the name. "She has a shop in town and runs one of those ghost tours. I've been on it a few times."

"Steve was talking about that girl? Jenna? What did he say? I never got a chance to talk to him before the battle."

"He said she plays a mean fiddle." Jake grinned, his eyes flashing. "And she has blue eyes, long blond hair, real pretty. And she's studying history. And she lives in Pennsylvania. Oh, I can't remember what else."

"Pennsylvania?" That didn't make sense. Miranda lived in Ramsey, Jenna's father lived in Pennsylvania. "Oh, her father's a lawyer in Pennsylvania. Her mother did say they were divorced, so the girl must move back and forth."

"Tough break," Jake said. His voice faded again. He reached down and picked a pebble from the dirt and twirled it thoughtfully between his fingers. He was looking at the little stone but not seeing it. "Went through that myself, a few years ago. No children, though, thank God. That would have made it worse than it was."

"Sorry, Jake. I didn't know." I half heard him. My mind was centering on a little bit of trivia he had mentioned. It rolled around inside my thoughts, getting louder each time. The train raid wasn't on the Web site.

..*one man is seen wandering around his farm.*

He shrugged, as though it wasn't as big a deal as it really was. "Happened a long time ago. Being the wife of a mailman wasn't quite good enough for her. Sorry. Letter carrier. It didn't have enough prestige for her. Can't really blame her none. It isn't exactly a glamorous career. And what's worse, I don't have the legs for wearing those shorts. Too skinny." He tried to smile but fell short. "Funny, but growing up I never thought of being a mailman. Wasn't one of my career choices. I just fell into it, and its good money, but it wasn't what I had in mind, not one of my dreams. Now it's too late to change. And she's remarried anyway. Years ago. Didn't take her long, either. New husband, kids now. A whole new family." The family he should have had, he seemed to say.

"Sorry, Jake." I tried to concentrate on his words, tried to ignore the echo in my mind. The train raid wasn't on the Web site. "What would you have done if you didn't become a letter carrier?"

His head shook slowly back and forth. "Old dreams, Frank. I don't even want to dust 'em off."

"Yeah, but what was it you wanted to do when you were a kid?"

He smiled then and nodded toward the tents surrounding us. "I'm doing it, Frank, I'm doing it. So, does this stuff about the company history have anything to do with what happened this afternoon?"

The train raid wasn't on the Web site.

It was bad enough I had hallucinated a phantom regiment and that probably the entire encampment knew about it. I was not about to tell anyone about the train raid and the murders of Union prisoners. Not that I couldn't deal with ridicule. I was, after all, a high school teacher. But something bugged me about that particular hallucination, something that could not be simply explained away with heat exhaustion.

"I can't imagine seeing what you saw," Jake went on.

Yes, that train raid was disturbing. It had seemed so real, especially … and my mind flashed with the incident two months ago, in the boys' lavatory. That had not been a hallucination, the boy had not been a specter. I had prayed that it hadn't been real, that it had been a creation of my imagination. I would give anything if that had been an illusion.

"I've been all over the place," he continued, "to battlefields, cemeteries, all sorts of places, even those ghost tours, and I've never seen anything like that. Not even close. Not at Gettysburg or Richmond, Sharpsburg or Harper's Ferry. Nothing. What was it like, Frank?"

"Ah, disturbing." I forced my breathing to steady. I looked down at my hands. They were clammy with perspiration and shaking.

"Jeeze, I never saw anything, let alone in the middle of the day. That just blows my mind. Too bad you were the only one who saw that ghost regiment."

"Oh, no." I waved my hands. "Not ghosts. I keep telling you, they weren't ghosts. Just my brain going haywire. Why do you think they appeared in broad daylight and only to me? They weren't real. I'm cracking up, that's all."

My voice had gained volume as I spoke, and I realized that some people, both tourists and reenactors, had stopped and stared. Even Doc had stopped his lecture to glance over.

Steve strolled into camp. "Still talking about that, huh Dad?"

I lowered my head into my hands. "Nice to see you're so concerned about your old man's sanity."

"Or lack thereof," he said.

I peeked through my fingers and saw him grinning. I tried not to laugh.

"You coming tonight?" he asked.

I lowered my hands and stared at him. I was looking forward to crawling into our tent early, hiding under my blanket, and trying to get as good a night's sleep as possible while lying on lumpy straw on top of lumpier ground. Ground that had been a battlefield a century and a half ago, where thousands had died. More fodder for my dreams, as though my subconscious needed more disturbing material. Suddenly sleep didn't look that appealing

Great. No wonder I was hallucinating.

"Where are you going?" I asked.

"Ramsey Mansion," he said as though I should have known. "The ball tonight? Remember?"

"Ah, yeah, but we've never gone to any of those before. Why the sudden interest?"

He shuffled his feet in the dirt. "Ah, well, you know. Jenna's going to be there, and I thought you'd like to hear her play."

Jake grinned at us. "The kid's only thinking of you, Frank. You know how you love that fiddle music."

"Yeah, I guess I forgot that. Okay, let's get cleaned up." At least the music might settle my nerves, a more appealing prospect than lying on the cold ground, staring at the tent ceiling, and trying to sleep without dreaming.

Jake got up to join us. "Sounds like a good idea. Do you know some of the history of the mansion? Mrs. Ramsey, a young bride, killed herself from sorrow over her husband's death at Chancellorsville. Actually, it's rumored that the elder Mr. Ramsey killed her. That's just one of the stories."

He rambled on and I tuned him out. Great. I wasn't going to escape my imagination running wild. With my brain turning to mush, I could dream up almost any sort of hallucination in a huge house full of tragic histories. My tent and bed of straw might prove more relaxing after all. What bothered me the most was that the train raid information had not been on the company's Internet page. I could not have read about it anywhere else. So how did my imagination create an hallucination of an actual event that I had no knowledge of?

Chapter Four

He discovereth deep things out of darkness, and bringeth out to light the shadow of death ... Job 12:22

The Ramsey family had lent their name to the town that had sprung up from the corners of their plantation. They had been among the first of those who had come to Virginia from England and had eventually settled on this land and built their homes and lives here. An earlier house had burned to the ground, replaced by the present mansion that sat opposite the Pine Creek Battlefield. Where the mansion had once looked out upon the dirt road dividing the plantation from the rolling, rock-strewn hills and tree-lined stream, it now witnessed a macadam highway and a small brick visitor's center. According to the battlefield brochures, those hills were much the same as they had been a hundred and fifty years ago. Down that road, the little town had spawned from the railroad and had also changed little, except maybe for the McDonalds and the Seven-Eleven and a few other more modern businesses. The land that stretched behind the mansion had once seen vast crops of cotton, tobacco, and wheat and in more recent times had been divided and portioned off for clusters of ranch houses and split-levels. In the forties, the mansion had fallen into disrepair during an economical downfall of the owner, a member of a branch of the Ramsey family. The local bank eventually took over ownership, rented it to a variety of failing businesses, sold off the land around it for housing development, and eventually turned the mansion into a museum with the partnership of the town's administration in order to attract tourism.

The patio and the gardens to the rear of the house were restored in the seventies and kept up by the Daughters of the Confederacy, and were the scene of this evening's ball. Surrounded by blossoms filling the senses, women in hoop gowns and men in dress uniforms once more strode the stones and pathways. The difference now was that uniforms of gray and blue mixed without confrontation. If any ghostly visitor of the past happened to witness the event, they would have been severely confused.

I thought of mentioning this paragon to Steve and Jake, but my son was preoccupied with finding his new friend, Jenna, and I hesitated to get Jake started on his paranormal discussion once more. So I simply stood in the background and listened to the music produced by the Logan Guard musicians from Pennsylvania and quietly contemplated the irony of a Northern band playing at a Southern mansion.

The evening was early, so the sun was still high above the mountains in the west. Electric lamps disguised to look like gas lamps hung around the garden for later, when the sun set. The discrepancy with period fixtures could be forgiven for the sake of safety.

Already dozens of people wandered the garden, a number attempting to dance on the patio, the metal on the bottom of the men's shoes clanking like horses' hooves. The women wore their finest gowns of every color and texture, with hats and plumes and fans. The men wore either civilian suits or uniforms. Against the shiny brass and decorations of those uniforms, my old shell jacket and trousers were shabby. I tried to blend into the background, but no one really cared. Although the officers in their dress uniforms with glistening sabers dangling at their sides stole the show, many lowly enlisted men in clothes adorned only with stains and tears took to the dance floor.

I spotted the tables laden with sandwiches, fruits, and desserts and made a straightforward assault. Apparently the lighting wasn't the only concession to modern technology; paper plates and cups were set out for our convenience rather than china or tin. That was fine with me, as long as I could have my fill.

Jake joined me and we watched the increasing crowd along with some modern tourists who freely snapped pictures.

Jake nudged me. "Look who's here."

Charlie had put on his best shell jacket and was chatting with two young Southern belles. They were laughing at one of his stories and sipping on punch from little paper cups.

"He doesn't waste any time," I said.

"He's really begging for trouble. If his wife catches wind of what he's been up to…"

I took a bite from a quarter wedge of a ham sandwich. "Are they having problems?"

Jake frowned. "They will pretty soon. He's always been like this, but I think it's getting worse. It used to be an occasional flirt, now he's at it all the time. It might seem innocent, but he's going too far. His wife is bound to hear about him carrying on. She'll leave him for sure."

I recalled what Jake had mentioned earlier about his own marital problems. I could tell it upset him to see a friend willing to throw away a good relationship just for the sake of a few moments of aimless flirting.

He shook his head. "What a jerk. Someone should give him a good kick in the butt and shake up his brains."

"You're the captain, Captain," I said. "That's why you get to wear all that gold on your uniform."

He lifted his arm to gaze at the swirl of rank insignia on the cuff of his jacket. "Yeah. Guess it's up to me."

The reluctance in his voice told me that he was not about to confront Charlie. If the opportunity arose, I might have a talk with him, though my recent attempts at counseling have had disastrous results. I would probably make things worse and be the cause of a major divorce trial. At the very least I'd be blamed for the separation and destroy a friendship.

The captain of Company H spoke briefly with Jake while passing over the buffet table. He gave me a curious look before moving on with a laden plate. He apparently recalled my unusual behavior on the field that afternoon and decided to give me a wide berth. Whether it was because he thought I had cracked up in battle or if he had heard what I believed I had seen, I wasn't sure. What's worse, having people believe you are crazy or that you see ghosts?

I nodded a greeting to General Robert E. Lee as he came to the table for a cup of punch. He smiled warmly in reply, nodded back, then moved off to talk with General Pickett and General Grant. Grant puffed on a thick cigar, sending a wreath of smoke around the brim of his slouch hat. Pickett twisted the tip of his mustache between thumb and finger. Presidents Lincoln and Davis discussed an event near Richmond earlier this year, sharing a laugh, stopping to put on serious expressions for a tourist to snap a picture.

General Longstreet, also smoking a cigar, stood with another Confederate general whom I could not place. His trim beard was liberally streaked with gray. He was in his late fifties, tall, narrow, and distinguished. He carried himself like a commanding officer or a natural leader.

"Who's that?" I asked Jake.

"Don't know. He doesn't look familiar." He shoved a sandwich wedge into his mouth. "I don't know who he's supposed to be," he mumbled around the sandwich.

"Beauregard?" I asked, taking a stab as though I actually knew these historical figures.

"Nah. The beard's all wrong."

"That uniform's never been on the field," I pointed out. "Or even on a horse. Looks like he hardly wears it."

"Some guys have uniforms just for parades and occasions like this." Jake was wearing his dressier jacket, which he reserved for parades. It still showed signs of wear. He squinted, then frowned. "He does look familiar, now that I think of it, but I still can't place him. I mean him, not his impression. He probably just dresses up for show. Just a farb."

"Oh," I said. Jake knew military history and personalities and reenactors, the serious ones and the farbs; I knew animal behavior, anatomy, and so on. I was out of my element. So I shoved a sandwich into my own mouth and contemplated searching for more.

Jake shook his head, then turned with me to the buffet table for our second assault.

"Why Mister Blaine, I thought you would have asked me for a dance."

I spun at the voice and found Miranda Connor inches from me. As I turned, my feet rustled the hem of her hoop gown. She no longer dressed in the personae of a gypsy but more like a Southern belle, all in bright blue. She waved her fan and the only thing that dangled from her wrist was a small velvet purse.

"We seem to be bumping into each other," she said with a coy smile and a tilt to her head.

Why hadn't I thought she would be here? Her daughter was here, and would later perform with the band, but her presence never crossed my mind. Now, I wished I had stayed in camp and gone to bed early, as I had planned. I battled the urge to look for a hole to crawl into.

"Nice to see you again, Mrs. Connor," I said and hoped my insincerity wasn't as obvious to her as it was to me.

She waved her fan at me. "Oh shush, you can call me Miranda. After all, our children are becoming good friends. And you don't mind me calling you Frank, do you?"

"Ah, not at all."

Jake wandered closer, his cheeks puffed out with a mouthful of something from the buffet. I quickly motioned to him.

"Ah, this is Jake Boden, our captain. Jake, Miranda Connor."

He swallowed hard so he could speak. "A pleasure, ma'am," he said as he touched the ends of her fingers. He had dropped into an accent that mirrored Miranda's. Every inch a Confederate gentleman. "I've visited your shop on occasion. And I've been on your midnight tours."

"Please come again, Captain. You're welcome any time," she said with a nod of appreciation. She leaned closer and lowered her voice. "One never knows what will happen on one of our tours. Sometimes nothing unusual, sometimes something quite unexpected."

I glanced around for an easy escape. I hated to retreat from the buffet, but I could always come back. Steve stood with Jenna near the Logan Guard, where they sat in a cluster of chairs on one side of the garden. Jenna had her fiddle out, fingers plucking it to tune it, and Steve held the case for her. I thought of making my way to them, maybe stand with Steve to listen to the music. But Miranda had other plans. Her hand fell across my arm.

"Frank? How about that dance?"

I forced a smile. "Sorry, but I don't dance." Except with my wife. "And I couldn't fake these steps."

"Oh, come now, Frank. I can teach you. You'll do fine. A few minutes of practice, and you'll dance as well as anyone here. Besides, have you seen how awful some of them are? Dreadful."

"Thank you, but no," I said, still trying to stay polite but beginning to wonder why I bothered. I nodded toward Jake, who had just shoved another sandwich into his mouth. "I'm sure the captain would be happy to. You both seem to have a similar interest in the supernatural."

Jake froze in mid-chew.

Miranda twirled on him. "Really? How interesting. I had offered to do a reading for Frank, but he's been reluctant. He doesn't even seem interested in one of our tours. But I think we can convince him. Did you know that the Ramsey House is on the tour? This is a very active place. I just shudder with all the energy surging on these grounds."

She curled her hand around Jake's right arm and then snagged my left before I could make a strategic retreat. Jake continued chewing and nodded enthusiastically.

"Did you know about Mrs. Rebecca Ramsey?" she asked, her tone hushed as though she didn't want to be overheard, but we weren't near anyone. "Tragic story. She was so young and beautiful, the daughter of a rich ship owner in Savannah. Young James Ramsey was an officer in the Virginia militia, graduate of VMI. A few weeks after their marriage, he went off to war. He died in the battle at Chancellorsville, and she died soon after that. She was terribly heartbroken. Officially, she committed suicide, but there were rumors of murder. Her father-in-law was not a nice person, nothing like poor James. Why she stayed here and did not return to her own family in Georgia, I just don't know. Very tragic. She's a well-known visitor here, ever since her death. She never actually left the estate."

"Have you ever seen her?" I asked.

"No," she said. "But many tourists have. And the museum's assistant director has seen her a number of times. Usually there are other manifestations, like doors closing or opening on their own, objects moved to different places in the house."

"But you haven't seen her," I insisted.

She finally got my intent and glared at me, her smile fading. "No, I haven't had the pleasure," she said tightly. "But I have experienced other visitations and other phenomena whenever I visit Ramsey House."

"Such as?" I asked. If I could trip her up, expose her superstitions for the fallacies they were, she might leave me alone out of irritation.

She stopped suddenly, pulling both Jake and me to a halt. Cold air rushed over me, chilling me. A moment ago I had been sweating beneath my shell jacket, perspiration covering my brow. The sunlight was beginning to fade as the sun touched the tops of the mountains, but the temperature had given no sign of dropping for a cooler, more comfortable evening. But at this moment, when Miranda snapped us to a stop, a chill filled the air, as though we had just stepped into a large walk-in freezer.

Miranda stepped back, dragging us with her.

And the hot humidity fell heavy on me.

She pulled us forward again, and we were surrounded by the dry coolness. One corner of her mouth curled up at me in a sarcastic, self-satisfied grin.

"Such as this," she said triumphantly. "A cold spot."

Chapter Five

For the morning is to them even as the shadow of death: if one know them, they are in the terrors of the shadow of death ... Job 24:17

Jenna Connor's fiddle spun its web through the garden, overpowering the rest of the band. The dancers paraded across the patio, following the directions of the instructor, tripping up occasionally, but generally having fun. I evaded Miranda's attempts at bringing me into one of the dances and was able to slide away along the ring of spectators to join Steve near the band. Miranda finally gave up on me and ensnared the tall, thin Confederate general we had seen earlier with General Longstreet. Miranda definitely knew the steps and her energy outshone anyone there. Her contagious laughter sparked the others into enjoying the evening.

"Nice music," I said to Steve as I watched the dancers trying to learn the old steps. Most were watching Miranda, taking their cue from her as well as the instructor.

"Yeah, great." He spent more of his attention on the fiddle player, but his eyes at least did wander now and then to the dancers and even to other members of the band.

Jake came up behind us and began telling Steve about our encounter with the cold spot. He bounced on his feet with excitement. "After all this time, I finally experience something supernatural. It isn't as interesting as seeing an apparition, but then it's a start. Who knows, maybe we'll encounter a visitation. Miranda seems to think you have been touched, Frank."

"Yeah," I said, then tapped the side of my head. I quite agreed with that. "I'm definitely touched."

"No, I mean supernaturally. She says there's something about your aura, that she even had a premonition of your coming this weekend."

I opened my eyes wide in mock surprise. "Really? Did her familiars mention me by name?"

"Ah, no, I don't think so. But I think she knew something strange was going to happen this weekend to someone in particular, and you fit the bill. I'm just glad I was along when we passed through that cold spot."

"Come on, Jake," I said, starting to lose my good humor. "There's a logical explanation for that, I just haven't figured it out. It was probably some atmospheric fluctuation. I'm a biologist, not a meteorologist. There just isn't anything supernatural."

"You know," Steve said, managing to tear his eyes from the fiddle player, "I've heard of cold spots, too, but I think they go along with my own theory of what's been happening."

"Oh, that your old dad is just burnt out, fried neurons and all," I said.

"No. Actually, I think it's a temporal disturbance. I don't believe in ghosts either."

Jake wagged his finger. "There's a lot of strange things in the world, and there's a supernatural as well as a natural. You, Frank, deal with the natural. So you don't understand the supernatural."

"I believe in the supernatural," Steve said. "And so does Dad. Right, Dad?"

"No," I said slowly, wondering what his point was.

"Sure you do. Well, not the supernatural the way it's popularized, the way Jake means," Steve went on, "but the spiritual world. Not ghosts. I mean God, and angels. Angels are spiritual beings, not physical. So there's a spiritual world just like a physical world. But I don't think the men Dad saw are spiritual, and definitely not ghosts. I think they're images out of the past. Somehow we get to see the past through temporal rifts. Sometimes they look solid, sometimes you can see right through them, depending on how strong the rift is. And that cold spot, I bet it was a place where a rift was forming. Maybe sometimes you don't see anything, just experience the opening of the rift."

"You mean we could have stepped through this hole and gone through time?" Jake was sucking all this in.

Steve shook his head. "Naw. They're too weak. We can only see images. Like with a TV. We get a picture, but the actors aren't transported into our living room. It's all very logical and goes along with modern quantum physics."

"Since when did you study quantum physics?" I asked, folding my arms over my chest. He barely passed trigonometry. A major in history was one way of avoiding undergraduate math classes.

He passed me one of those teenage looks of exasperation. "Dad, I watch the Discovery Channel sometimes."

"Okay, Professor Einstein," I said, reciprocating with my own middle-aged father look. "If what I saw marching into us was one of these temporal distortion images, then why was I the only one who saw it?"

He shrugged. "You were probably the only one in just the right spot at just the right time."

"I didn't feel any cold spot, either." And I would have noticed something like that in that heat.

"Frank," Jake said, his face sober, "it was either what Steve said, or you hallucinated or you saw a ghost regiment. Me, I opt for the ghost regiment. It's more exciting and it doesn't hurt the brain when you try to rationalize it with quantum physics."

I contemplated the three options, but I rejected Jake's standpoint immediately. I could not believe in ghosts, so either I hallucinated or Steve's theory was right. Or there was something none of us had yet considered. Still, of the present choices, only one was comforting.

"Good theory, Einstein," I told Steve, slapping him on the shoulder. Quantum temporal disturbance sounded better every minute.

Jake hung his head for a moment. "I don't know. Sounds good and all, but I don't know if it can explain every supernatural event. Besides, it makes ghosts sort of … dull. I mean, just pictures out of the past isn't very scary. It's like looking through a quantum photo album."

"Makes you feel a whole lot better after you've seen a few hundred of them marching right into you," I said. I didn't bother mentioning the vision of the train raid, but Steve's theory explained how I could see an event I knew nothing about. I hadn't read about the raid, so how could I hallucinate it? Maybe I saw it through a quantum window of time.

"Good point," Jake conceded. He looked around, his eyes catching on the buffet table. "Right now, I'm hungry. You guys can carry on your lesson in quantum physics—I'm going to snatch some more food."

He started directly toward the buffet, but stopped, spun around and walked back. He flashed a weak smile as he passed us. We watched him circle the patio and the crowd of energetic dancers now in pursuit of a waltz. Steve and I glanced at each other, shrugged, then watched Jake as he flanked the buffet table. It was literally a roundabout way of getting to it, a three-hundred-sixty-degree plan of attack.

"Ah!" I cried as I realized Jake's rationale. I pointed to just this side of the buffet. "That's about where the cold spot was. Our Captain Jake decided to avoid another encounter with it. He was anxious for a supernatural experience, but he's not thrilled for a repeat. Or maybe your theory makes him more nervous than the ghosts. He may not have been comforted with your suggestion that the rift is too weak to step through." I looked at Steve. "You really believe that whole temporal thing?"

"Sure, Dad. It makes perfect sense. And it's scientific. It's all a matter of quantum, on a sub-atomic level—"

"You're making that all up," I said.

"Naw. It was on the Discovery Channel."

"You sure? You wouldn't lie to your old man?"

"Never!" He held up his hand as though to swear in court, but the corners of his mouth quivered. He couldn't quite hold back a chuckle.

"I knew it," I said.

"You used to be a scientist, Dad. Doesn't it make sense?"

Children have a way of making you feel so successful, intelligent and proud. This was not one of those times. "Yeah," I said with little enthusiasm. Used to be … thanks a lot, kid. And you used to wear diapers and eat strained beets.

The subject fell by the wayside, and we listened to the music once more. Our silence felt awkward, and I wanted to bring up a different subject. The last one left me uneasy.

"Have you seen Badger?" I asked.

Steve shook his head, still trying to watch Jenna swing her bow.

"I saw him leave camp before we did," I said. "I thought he might be on his way over here, but I haven't seen him."

Steve shook his head again. "Haven't seen him. I see Charlie over there, dancing with that blonde from the Union camp. Isn't she a bit young for him? I think she's my age."

I hadn't thought he would notice anyone beyond his favorite musician. His powers of observation were as startling as his powers of reasoning. "Too young or not, he's married."

"Maybe you should have a talk with him. You're good at that."

I shot him a glance, but his attention was elsewhere. He really didn't know all that had happened two months earlier, and I never told him. I couldn't tell anyone. I could argue about my ability to give anyone advice, but that might bring up the question of why. I couldn't go into it, especially with him. I just let the comment fall on the bricks of the patio and we lapsed into silence once more.

I wandered off, leaving Steve to enjoy the music, or the musician. Before I left the garden, the song ended and Jenna joined him. I'd give him some space, and keep an eye on him from a respectable distance.

The music had died away, but now the conversation rose as dancers and spectators mingled in the garden, talking and laughing. Jake was in friendly conversation with the captain from Company H.

I walked through the French doors into the house and began wandering through the rooms of the lower floor of the mansion. The large rooms were furnished with original furniture and decorations, many remnants of the Ramsey family. Some of their portraits hung in the expansive entranceway. The names beneath the paintings meant nothing to me, except that they were of the Ramsey lineage. I did catch one name, under a portrait of a young man wearing the uniform of a Confederate colonel. The plaque read James Elisha Ramsey. Here was the ill-fated young heir who had died in the battle of Chancellorsville and had left his young bride. Other visitors passed as I strolled along, and we greeted each other with friendly nods. After a while, I heard the music start up again. One couple who had been touring the hall left to either join in the dance or to listen to the band. I turned to go in order to see what Steve was up to. We needed to be leaving soon, in order to get a good night's sleep.

As I turned, I saw someone out of the right corner of my eye.

"Hi," I said.

The woman stepped closer, and at first I thought it was Miranda Connor. But this woman was younger, no more than twenty, though pale and thin. Her hair was brown, tied into a bun on the top of her head. Her gown was a pale blue, with a high collar and puffy, long sleeves, not the sort of dress that would be comfortable in this heat. A sweet lilac scent drifted up from her.

She didn't seem to be enjoying the party. Her expression was miserable, like someone who had lost something of importance. Given that and the lack of color in her face, I suspected she was sick.

"Are you all right, Miss?" I asked. After all, I knew how the heat could affect someone. I didn't know how those people could dance while wearing so many layers of clothes. It was a wonder nobody dropped over in the middle of the dance floor.

Her pale blue eyes looked at me without blinking. "He's waiting for you," she said.

Her voice was so low and light, I wasn't sure I heard her correctly. "Pardon?"

Her eyes flicked down the hall, toward the sounds of the music, then came back to me. "He's waiting for you."

"Who?" I asked. Maybe Steve was searching for me, and this young woman was trying to give me the message. Or Jake was looking for me. I had lost track of how long I had been in the house. Steve and Jake might be ready to leave.

I turned to look down the hall, but I couldn't see outside from that angle. When I turned back, I was alone in the hall. A puff of my breath condensed in the frigid air where the woman had been. She was gone.

I looked around, glanced into the nearest drawing room, then the library across the hall. No one. I never heard the swish of skirt and petticoat, nor the tap of shoe. My own steps echoed through the hall and up to the second floor, those metal horseshoes on my brogans making an awful racket in the silent house, like a Clydesdale trotting over the hard wood floors. I was still alone and had an overwhelming desire not to be so. Of course, there was a logical explanation for the woman's abrupt disappearance. I just couldn't come up with one.

On my way out, I stopped suddenly at the sight of the woman. Unfortunately, she was on one of the portraits hanging on the wall. The same small features, the same hairstyle. The brass label on the frame gave her name, but I thought the painting made Rebecca Ramsey's eyes a deeper blue. Her portrait hung next to that of her husband, James Ramsey.

So I just had a brief conversation with the tragically late Mrs. Ramsey. Had I known who she was, I might have inquired as to her death, in order to quell the debate as to suicide versus murder. Having met her, I tended toward murder by her treacherous father-in-law. She seemed strong-willed enough to weather the death of her husband without resorting to suicide, even though she appeared in great emotional pain. That could have been from her husband's death or her own. Although she was not an attractive woman, she was rather well preserved for being over a century and a half old.

The Logan Guard played once more as the dancers attempted another dance. This time, a reluctant Steve was in the middle of the perspiring, out-of-breath mass, receiving encouragement from Jenna. I found Jake, who had abandoned his raid on the buffet and idly watched the spectacle while tapping his foot to the music.

I came up beside Jake and said, "One of Steve's temporal anomalies just spoke to me."

Jake didn't turn my way immediately. After a few seconds, his foot froze in mid-tap. Slowly his head swiveled toward me. "You saw another one? Oh, man!" He sounded disappointed he had not been in on this one.

I nodded slowly. "The late, lamented Rebecca Ramsey."

"You're kidding! I knew there'd be something like this. Didn't I tell you about a visitation? I don't know how many times I've been here, I've never seen her. How did you know it was her? How close were you?"

"About as close as we are," I said. "Any closer and we could have danced the waltz. And I saw her portrait afterwards. That's how I knew it was her. Same sullen look, same hairstyle, different dress, though. Of course, I could have seen the portrait earlier and my subconscious blocked it out and created the illusion of her, but she was solid, three-dimensional. So maybe Steve's right."

"Wait! Did you say she spoke to you?" His eyes were on the verge of bugging out of their sockets.

"Yep. That tends to put a wrench in Steve's quantum leap theory. That's not just an image passing through a temporal rift. She looked as solid as you or I, and she spoke directly to me. She looked me in the eye, too. That's pretty much interaction."

Jake snatched his kepi off his head and raked his fingers through his hair, grabbing hold of his hair as he shook his head. "I told you that theory couldn't explain all the supernatural sightings or encounters. I guess you could modify the theory to include Mrs. Ramsey. We can talk to Steve, see what he thinks."

I eased out a sigh. "Jake, he just graduated high school, not MIT."

"Well then you saw a ghost." He looked triumphant.

"I didn't see a ghost." My voice rose sharply. Several heads turned in my direction. I felt my face heat up. I tugged on the sleeve of Jake's uniform and led him further away from the crowd around the patio. My mind had fallen into a fog of shock and struggled to burst free to find some semblance of rationality. She could not have been a ghost; she could not have been the actual Rebecca Ramsey. There was a logical explanation, if not Steve's temporal rift. "Jake, there are no ghosts. Someone around here might have a bizarre sense of humor and dressed up like Mrs. Ramsey. After all, there's Lee and Grant over there getting their picture taken, and I saw Lincoln drive up today in an SUV. This whole town has people dressed like historical figures. Why can't someone do the same for the sake of the Ramsey House museum? She probably either works here or got hired because she has a passing resemblance to Mrs. Ramsey's portrait. She might even be out there dancing."

Jake glanced out at the dancers. I didn't bother, since I didn't want to be proven wrong. The threads of reality that I clung to were fraying. The woman had effectively vanished from the hall without a sound. I couldn't explain that. Was this one more step to losing my mind?

"What did she say to you?" Jake asked. "Did she say something like, 'Welcome to the Ramsey Mansion?' Or did she run through the hours the house is open to the public?"

His sarcasm wasn't appreciated, and I really didn't want to tell him, but I did. "'He's waiting for you.'"

"Jake, there are no ghosts."

"That's it?"

"Well, she said it twice. I wasn't sure I heard her the first time."

"Who's waiting?"

I shrugged. "That's what I asked her. She seemed to mean someone out here. She looked toward the garden."

"Did she answer you?" he asked. He looked around as though he might either catch sight of her or the person she was talking about.

"She never got the chance. She disappeared before she could."

Jake jabbed his thumb toward Steve and Jenna, twirling through the steps of the dance. "Could she have meant Steve?"

"Jake, either she wasn't real or it was a person dressed up to look like Rebecca Ramsey. She couldn't have meant ..."

I had looked over to watch Steve in his miserable attempt at dancing with Jenna. Despite the girl's patience, her instructions just were not sinking in. They didn't care. They were both laughing, hands clasped in an approximation of the stance. Others around them were also laughing at their own problems, and more than one couple had difficulty getting the steps right. On the other side of the patio, though, I caught sight of a familiar face. There, with his dark eyes on me, stood the Union colonel I had seen on the train. A smile formed beneath his drooping mustache and he dipped his slouch hat toward me.

"Jake!" I grabbed his arm so hard he jumped. "Do you see that man over there? Union officer, slouch hat?"

He squinted. "Big mustache?"

"Yeah. You see him?" I held my breath. Was it possible I wasn't hallucinating?

"Sure. But he doesn't look much like Rebecca Ramsey."

I was about to explain he was the one I had seen on the train, but I then realized I had not told anyone about that particular hallucination. I closed my mouth and tried to think of a reason why this particular man might disturb me.

"He looks familiar," I said lamely.

The man continued to watch me. A chill ran through me. I had to get to him, see what he wanted, see if he was real. Jake could see him, so he must be real. Maybe I hadn't hallucinated, and maybe someone was messing with my mind, playing a cruel prank. If this guy was real, then Mrs. Ramsey was real. And they had a way of making it look like they disappeared. I had to talk to this man.

I ran the circumference of the garden, trying to keep my eye on the enigmatic colonel. He turned with me, following me with his eyes. Once I made it to the other side of the garden, I pushed my way through the spectators toward the front. The last couple parted, and ...

No one.

"How does he keep doing that!" I snapped.

I received a number of malevolent stares from the people around me, especially from those I had shoved aside. I looked around, jumped up and down, and generally made more of a fool of myself in trying to locate the man. Jake was on the other side of the garden. I waved my arms to get his attention, then lifted my hands up in question. Had he seen the man? He shook his head, then shrugged.

The music stopped and the exhausted dancers fell into weary laughter. I passed among them on my way toward Jake. I neared Steve, laid my hand on his shoulder, then went on. He and Jenna trailed behind me. When I joined Jake, I found he had company.

Miranda Connor grinned at me. "So, I hear y'all met the lady of the manor."

I passed a scowl at Jake. "Or a reasonable facsimile," I said.

She took my arm with one hand and patted it with the other. "Now Frank, don't deny it. You should be honored. She doesn't make an appearance for just anyone, and I knew you were special when we first met."

"You saw what?" Steve asked, but I had to ignore him for the moment. Jake sidled up to him and described my recent encounter while I concentrated on Miranda.

"Now wait a minute. I'm sure that was someone dressed up like Rebecca Ramsey. She's probably still around here."

Her grin widened. "Oh, she's still here, honey. She's been here for a hundred and fifty years. You can ask the museum staff, if you want, but no one impersonates Mrs. Ramsey. Just accept it that you met her. Do you mind if I mention this on my tour? And did she actually speak to you? Your handsome Captain Boden told me all about it. You're doubly honored, Frank Blaine. Usually she just appears at a distance, on the stairs or in the garden. This has been quite an evening."

"That's not all," Jenna said, without any trace of a Virginian accent. She must have spent most of her time with her father. "Mr. Blaine saw a whole regiment on the battlefield this afternoon. Steve told me."

"Really?" She dragged the word out as she turned from her daughter to me. "And you never mentioned it. Shame on you, Frank. Now, you must tell me everything, and I insist on you allowing me to tell everyone on my tour. You've never been in Ramsey before, and here you've had two encounters, all in the same day. Why, it makes me wonder what tomorrow might be like."

I disengaged my arm and said sharply, "Now listen, I saw ... someone. Not a ghost. And as far as those soldiers are concerned, the heat affected me. I hallucinated. I didn't see any ghost. If anything, it was a temporal ... thingy." I waved my hands toward Steve.

"Anomaly," he said.

"Right. So that's it. End of story." I folded my arms over my chest to emphasize that I was finished with this conversation.

"Of course," Miranda said as though appeasing a child. "Now, what did Rebecca say to you?"

"'He's waiting for you,'" Jake said, happy to be of assistance.

I glared at him.

Miranda tapped the polished nail of her index finger to her lips. "Really? That's fascinating. Any idea who she meant?"

Before I could even refuse to talk, Jake said, "There was some strange guy in a colonel's uniform over there before the dance ended. He was looking at Frank, but he slipped away before Frank could get to him."

"You saw him, too?" she asked.

He nodded, then grinned. "Was he a ghost too?" He sounded like a child who had caught his first sight of Santa.

Miranda frowned. "I don't remember hearing about anyone like that. The house has been used as a command post as well as a hospital. There had been reports of officers being seen in the living room and some appearances in various bedrooms. We could examine the old photographs in the house and the Ramsey portraits."

I turned away from them. They were all being ridiculous. This whole incident had been blown out of proportion. From my heat-induced hallucinations to some woman in period dress, all this was easily explained and I refused to fuel their delusions. It was time to get back to camp, and I wished I had never come over. I would give them some time, then I'd collect Steve. The paths through the garden provided some solitude. I stomped along them to escape. I didn't want to hear anything more about ghosts or temporal anomalies or hundred and fifty-year-old murders. I needed to put some distance between Miranda Connor and myself, or I might blow up and say something unkind. I was growing tired of her supernatural trash.

The voices of the crowd dwindled. I passed a couple of other people strolling through the garden, each of us nodding and smiling amiably. My own smile was tight and artificial. Had I spoken I probably would have snapped some poor guy's head off.

The man stood under an elm, the brim of his slouch hat shadowing his face in the gloom feebly broken by the distant patio lights. He dipped his hat toward me.

I wanted to throttle him. He represented all the trouble of the day, since it began with my first sight of him on that train.

"Well," I said, unable to keep the anger out of my voice, "care to explain yourself?"

He leaned against the trunk of the elm, so at ease that he looked like he owned the place. He looked solid enough. Maybe if I slapped him I could prove to both of us that he was real.

"What do you want?" I demanded.

"Much."

His voice was low, barely audible over the murmurs from the fading party. His mustache bounced as he spoke, but his mouth remained invisible underneath.

"Very funny," I said. "Tell me, Colonel, are you real or just a figment of my fevered imagination?"

He straightened and faced me, but I still couldn't make out much of his features. "I am what I am, sir."

"That doesn't help. I'd suggest you were caused by a piece of undigested beef, but I didn't eat much today. So I won't bother suggesting that you're more gravy than grave. Care to get to the point and explain what you want?"

"Retribution."

"Stop being so cryptic," I snapped. "I'm not in the mood."

He shrugged. "We shall meet on the field of honor, sir."

"No good," I said. "Listen, Colonel Marley, I'm getting tired of you and your friends playing with me. Playtime's over, okay? Understand?"

"Men from your company were responsible for the murders of several Union soldiers," he said, his voice hinting at a New England accent. "We will meet and exact retribution for the atrocity."

"You're taking this way too seriously, mister."

I turned to go back down the path, and he was standing in front of me. "How did you do that?" I demanded.

He chose to ignore my question. "We shall meet on the field of honor,

Sunday before dawn. And you shall join the rest of your comrades."

Before I could grab hold of him, he turned and walked down the path toward the party. I hurried after him, but found myself alone on the path as it emptied onto the patio flooded with the lights. Fewer people scattered over the patio, but I could not see anyone resembling the Union colonel. He was gone again.

"Ah, Frank!"

Miranda glided toward me, followed by her daughter and my son. The Confederate general she had danced with earlier was at her side, their arms entwined.

"Frank, I would like you to meet someone."

Well, at least this guy was solid. She was touching him. He untangled himself from her and reached out his hand toward me. I took it and felt reassured at its warmth and strength.

"Malcolm Merryweather," he said, his voice as strong as his handshake.

"Frank Blaine," I replied. "Nice to meet you." As long as he didn't disappear when I turned away.

"My daughter has been telling me about you," he said.

"Your daughter?" I must have stared at him as I wondered who he was talking about and why she had been talking about me. Was he a key to that woman pretending to be Rebecca Ramsey?

Miranda curled her arm around the man's. "Daddy is fascinated about such things. That's how I got my interest in my profession. I came to it honestly. Daddy would like to hear about your experiences."

"There isn't much to tell," I insisted. I wanted to grab Steve and get out of there.

"Nonsense," Merryweather said. "I'm interested in hearing your ideas on these experiences. Being a scientist, you are probably less inclined to attribute them to the supernatural. Surely you have some theories."

"My son does," I said.

"Good." He glanced over at Steve. "I insist that you both come to my home tomorrow, for lunch. Please, don't say no, Frank. May I call you Frank? I insist. My housekeeper is an excellent cook, and I imagine whatever she whips up will be an improvement over what might be on the menu at your camp. My granddaughter will also be there, I assure you."

Steve grinned and nodded hopefully.

"Thank you," I said, though my tone was tired and didn't sound very appreciative.

"Just come to our tent tomorrow, Frank," Miranda said, obviously pleased, "and I'll explain how to get there. We could ride together, if you like."

I thanked them again, hoping I sounded a little more enthusiastic, and made my goodnights. I pushed Steve toward the garden's exit and breathed a sigh of relief as we clomped across the highway toward the Pine Creek Battlefield. Tiny lights dotted the field from many campfires and lanterns.

"Where's Jake?" I asked.

"He went back. We couldn't find any portrait or old photo that resembled that guy you and he saw, so he decided to head back to camp."

"I saw the guy again."

"Yeah?" He waited for me to continue.

"We had an interesting conversation. Seems he's upset about that train raid when the raiders killed off the Union soldiers and made off with the money."

"That's a long time to carry a grudge," he pointed out. "Was he for real?"

"I didn't poke him, tempted though I was, but he looked solid enough."

"Doesn't sound like a temporal image, does it?" he said.

I was about to agree with him when a red pickup rumbled over the path on the field, coming from the corner where the reenactors were permitted to park. The headlights blazed over us, and the driver hit the brakes. Bits of gravel rattled up into the undercarriage.

"Frank, Steve!"

The passenger door flew open and we saw Jake behind the wheel.

"What's up?" I asked. Taking the open door as an invitation, we climbed into the cab.

"It's Badger."

Chapter Six

Have the gates of death been open unto thee? Or hast thou seen the doors of the shadow of death? Job 38:17

Jake pulled his pickup into the gravel parking lot of the bar on the outskirts of Ramsey. A neon light glowed with the name Harley's, casting an eerie red haze over all the vehicles in the lot. This being Friday night, the parking lot was filled with at least a dozen other pickups and as many motorcycles. The building was low, dark, and small. Two small windows in the front held neon beer signs attached to plywood that completely blocked the windows. Other signs hung on the outside, looking like glow-in-the-dark graffiti. The door in the center was heavy steel with scars and dents. Two street lamps on either side of the lot threw a meager illumination on the place, giving the big neon sign on the roof little competition.

"What makes you think Badger's here?" I asked as we pulled in to face the rundown building.

"A couple of guys from one of the other companies saw him," Jake said. "They were on their way back to camp when I was coming back from Ramsey House. They said he was in pretty bad shape, though they weren't in the best condition themselves. I guess they'd been to a couple of other places in town and I don't think they stayed here long. Just in and out, and they noticed Badger. They've heard him preaching before and thought it was pretty funny to find him here with a bunch of bikers. I didn't share in their joke. It's a wonder they found their way back." He looked at the bar. "Ah, they didn't actually describe this place. I thought it was just a regular dive."

"I wouldn't know," I said. "The only dives I'm familiar with were in the ocean." I opened the door, then turned to Steve. I regretted bringing him along. I couldn't take him inside, especially since I didn't want to go in myself. I stabbed my finger at him. "You stay here. Keep the doors locked. You coming, Jake?"

Jake leaned forward to look at me while Steve scooted over to take my vacated seat. "I'll find a spot to park, then join you inside." He looked pale and he didn't sound very enthusiastic.

I nodded, then slammed the door shut.

Before I reached the front door, my feet felt the gravel vibrating from the noise from inside the bar. I pulled on the handle and the hinges screeched. The blast of country music at maximum volume nearly tossed me back. I forced my way through the thick atmosphere of cigarette smoke and stale odors while my ears stung from the blaring sounds thundering from the speakers of the glowing jukebox in one corner. In the smoky gloom, huge shapes hunkered—bikers, truckers, and locals of more colorful reputations. Laughter, grunts, and curses competed with the music. A few voices sang along with the jukebox.

I stood just inside the door to get my bearings and became aware of the nasty looks coming from half the clientele, but I've experienced that a few times in my career. An adult doesn't enter high school without getting nasty looks from the population, and there were always students who thought they could intimidate the staff the same way they could their classmates, especially if they were larger than the teachers. It never worked.

Badger sat at a table near the bar. His old friend Jewel hung over him in an attempt to rekindle their former friendship. Red sat next to him, his head pillowed by his entwined arms on the table. His breathing was deep and regular. Two other bikers sat on the other side. One was thin and cadaverous, his long, straggly beard trying ineffectually to hide pitted cheeks. He wore a black tee shirt from a Def Lepard tour. His arms, thin but tight with wiry muscles, were covered with tattoos that illustrated skulls and daggers in a number of combinations. The man next to him was as large as Badger, at least ten years younger, and without an ounce of body fat. His leather vest stretched over tight pectorals and threatened to tear at the seams with his every movement. His bulging biceps were so huge that shirt sleeves were not able to fit them. Only two places could produce such a sculptured body, the gym or the jail, and his clean-shaven, scarred face and the crooked nose suggested that he might not be a member of a gym. The biceps of his right arm rippled the image of a demonic dragon with a serpentine tail. The man's wavy dark hair was trimmed short, showing off his brown, chiseled features that hinted a Hispanic lineage. Empty beer bottles crowded the table, and each person, even Red, clutched a fresher bottle still holding some liquid.

As I approached the table a thicker odor assailed me. At least one person among them was in desperate need of a bath, and I suspected most of those present contributed to the smell. The clank of my shoes on the floor attracted more attention.

"Badger?" I said, trying to keep the apprehension out of my voice and trying desperately to come up with some plan. Why would Badger bother to listen to me, especially with his old friends surrounding him?

He looked up, his face stern and his eyes glaring. He didn't look like the same person, even though he still wore his cotton shirt and wool trousers with suspenders.

"You okay?" I asked. "Ready to go?" That sounded pretty lame.

The muscular biker took a swig of his beer, then slammed the bottle down with a bang that was meant as a warning. "What's it to you, *amigo*? You a cop?"

"No," I said, trying not to let fear enter my voice. I may have run across some big kids in high school, but none of them were this huge. They were easier to intimidate because of their youth and inexperience. This man's experience probably included a number of years in prison; chances were for a violent crime. I doubt those muscles were just for exhibition. He could have crushed my spine with one hand. I calmed my nerves and said, matter-of-factly, "I'm a teacher."

The skinny guy laughed and gulped some of his beer.

The big one grinned, showing off one gold tooth. "Teacher, eh? Not an English teacher. I hate English teachers. They always tellin' me what to do, what to say. They never like my accent. Spanish never good enough for them. You an English teacher?"

"No. Science."

His biceps rippled, bulging into rock-hard mountains. "Good. If you was an English teacher I'd have to beat the crap out of you."

"Lucky me. What do you beat out of me since I'm only a science teacher?"

He glared at me. "I give you a break."

"Which arm?" I asked, praying he wouldn't take me up on the suggestion. I felt the sweat trickle down the middle of my back.

He pursed his lips, then nodded. He still didn't look very happy. "You okay, professor. You Badger's *amigo*? Drag over a chair. I'm buying. They call me Diablo," he added with a flare to the name.

How fitting, I thought. I opened my mouth to politely decline the invitation.

"He ain't stayin'," Badger said.

Badger's eyes were cold, his jaw set tight. He gazed steadily at me. I had never seen him drunk, in fact I had never seen him drink alcohol of any kind, but he didn't look intoxicated. He wasn't a happy drinker. He looked ready for a fight. Even with Jewel nearly in his lap, her arms around him and fingers twirling his sweaty hair, he was not in good spirits. My impulse was to leave, and quickly. Badger obviously didn't want to go along with me, and I would never be able to bully him out of the bar. I might plead, but that would bring down ridicule from all the other patrons, most of whom still eyed me with malevolence. I couldn't appear weak, or I might not make it out on both feet. I glanced over my shoulder, hoping Jake would show up, though two Civil War reenactors were not much against a bar full of bikers and truckers.

The jukebox fell still, and no one spoke. Except for Red, who was either sleeping or unconscious, all eyes were on me, as though waiting for me to run along and bother someone else.

"It's getting late, Badger," I said, breaking through the silence, not willing to give up. But I was alone. Maybe I should have dragged all of the Thirteenth Virginia out of camp to help bring Badger back. Jake wouldn't be much back-up whenever he finally came in. He would at least look a little more imposing than I, with his height and rangy appearance. He must be having a hard time finding a parking space.

"The night's still young, ain't it, Badger," Jewel said with a sly smile. She nuzzled closer to him. "We got a lot of catchin' up to do."

Red groaned and lifted his head slightly.

"Go on back, Frank," Badger said.

"I've got your ride outside," I said. I wondered how I could make a graceful retreat.

"I'm not going," he said.

Diablo stood up, his chair scraping across the scarred wood floor. "Okay, professor, time to get lost. Badger ain't ready to leave."

This reminded me of a confrontation with a high school senior, a football player who had been stoned at the time he decided to become rebellious. He had been a head taller and fifty pounds heavier. I wondered if there was any parallel. This guy might be under the influence of a few beers and who knew what else, and he may have the intellect of an adolescent but the advantage of years of violence. Nope, no parallel.

"Hey man," Badger said. He waved a dismissive hand at the big man. "He's cool. Take it easy, Diablo. He'll leave." He turned to me, his thick brow furrowing. "Frank, get out. Go back to camp."

"Yeah," said the thin biker with a sneer, "go back to playing Civil War."

"Badger," I said, my voice drowned out by everyone's laughter. My face heated with embarrassment, fear, and anger. Anger was winning out, which was not a good thing in a place where the women were more muscular than I was. I waved my hands to encompass the table, his companions, and the bar in general. "Is this what you want?"

He glanced around, which looked more like an eye twitch rather than a pan to take in his surroundings. His eyes came back to me, but couldn't hold mine for more than a few seconds. His lips drew into a thin line beneath his beard. "Just get out, Frank."

I threw up my hands. "Okay. If that's what you want, okay. Just remember you've got friends back at camp. We're there for you when you need us." Now if I could just get out of the bar in one piece.

I turned and stared into the bulging chest of Diablo. He folded his arms and glared down at me. My inclination was to cower away from him and slink out with the help of shadows, but I stood my ground, ignoring the pounding in my chest and the rushing in my ears. I expected his fists to strike out at any moment and I wondered how much pain was involved in a broken nose or fractured jaw. Whatever happened I deserved for an overt expression of stupidity.

Diablo grinned, his gold tooth flashing, and took a single step sideways. He waved a hand toward the exit. "*Adios*, professor. Tonight, you are one lucky man."

When the door shut behind me, I started shaking. I tried to convince myself that the danger had been no greater than with any oversized teenager, but my imagination fell short. If I had shown any fear or hesitation, I may have been beaten, stabbed, or who knows what else, despite Badger's interference. There was still a possibility that Diablo or his friends might follow me out and teach me a lesson out of sight of Badger. I wanted to put as much distance between the bar and myself as quickly as possible and it was all I could do to not break into a full run. I had to find Jake's truck.

Considering there were over a dozen pickups in the lot, finding Jake's might not be so easy. I hurried through the lot, crunching gravel underfoot and looking into the cabs of each truck that resembled Jake's. The gloom that resulted from the distant streetlights added to the difficulty. I made my way to the one end of the lot with no luck. I had to pass the bar again to check out the other side. When the front door slammed open, I dropped down between two vehicles. I peeked over the hood of an old Buick to see two figures stagger out of the building. Neither was the scale of Diablo and they didn't look dangerous in the slightest.

Headlights flashed on a truck parked near the road. I crept closer, and when the truck appeared to resemble Jake's, my confidence grew. I approached it and saw a shadow in the passenger seat.

The door opened and the interior light flashed on, illuminating Steve.

"Where's Badger?" he asked.

"He doesn't want to come with us," I told him. "He's reminiscing with old friends. So ..." I looked around. "Where's Jake?"

Steve shrugged. "He went to give you a hand. We couldn't find a spot in the parking lot, so he had to park here along the road. He left about five minutes ago."

"He went inside?" Maybe I missed him, but he should have seen my encounter with Badger and his friends. Most of the bar patrons had been watching, especially when Diablo had stood to tower over me. They were probably disappointed there had been no fight ... yet. I looked toward the bar, but I couldn't see the front from that angle.

Steve shook his head. "Can't see the door from here. I only saw you skulking around the cars."

"I wasn't skulking."

I heard the gravel crunch behind me and my heart thumped heavily. I didn't want to turn to see Diablo's hulk bearing down on me, but I didn't want to be surprised by his attack, either. Jake had left the keys in the truck, but I would have to go the whole way around to get into the driver's side. Considering the approaching footfalls were close, I had no time to start the engine, let alone get into the truck. I balled my hands into fists and turned with the conviction that I would put up a good fight, and die with honor. Steve could at least drive off for medical help. I turned and came face to face with Jake.

"Here you are," he said needlessly, a big grin on his face.

"Yeah. I was wondering where you were."

"We must have missed each other. I saw Badger, but I didn't see you."

So, we really had missed each other. By the time he had parked and made it to the front door of the bar, I was probably wandering through the dark parking lot searching for his truck.

I shrugged. "There wasn't much you could have done. Badger doesn't want to come back with us."

"I was afraid of that." He frowned. "I wasn't quite sure what I expected when I headed out here. I didn't expect a place like this. What a dive." He glanced over his shoulder as though he expected one of the bar's denizens to sneak up on him and take exception to his referring to Harley's in such a way.

He froze, mouth agape, and I saw what he had seen. A lone figure lumbered toward us. He was large, broad, and tall. I immediately thought it was Diablo, come to wreak vengeance without the chance of Badger interfering. He appeared to be alone, though one or more of his friends could be coming at us from other angles. Our best chance was to get into the truck as fast as possible.

Jake and I scrambled toward the truck—he to the driver's door, me to the open passenger door, while the approaching mass slowly took shape, with shoulders not quite as broad as Diablo and a face bearing a thick beard.

"Can I bum a ride?" Badger asked gruffly.

I stopped as I was about to hurl myself up next to Steve. Jake had just swung his own door open. He stopped with his hand on the door, hung his head down, and breathed a deep sigh. My heart began to pound again.

I turned on him. "I thought you weren't coming back with us."

He made a sharp cut with one hand. "Let's not go there right now, Frank, okay?"

"Okay," Jake said, "let's get outta here." He climbed into the truck and started up the engine.

Badger went around me and climbed over the tailgate, settling in without another word.

*****

A few fires and lanterns speckled the darkness that blanketed the field. Voices were hushed. Most of the camp had retired to their respective tents. A harmonica played a few faint strains, a soft lullaby on the warm breeze, a sound out of time, welcoming us back to the nineteenth century.

Badger sat on a wooden camp chair, elbows on knees, head cradled in his hands. He stared into the fire as though trying to decipher the crackles and sparks. We had parked on the edge of the battlefield and walked the inky distance to our quarter of the camp in silence. Badger had lumbered along, hands shoved into his pockets, head hung low with his chin bouncing against his chest, a dark cloud surrounding him. He had sunk onto the chair near the fire and stayed there, without a word or sound to anyone. The rest of us puttered about the camp and readied for bed.

Sam wondered back into camp, his eyes sagging, a dejected look pulling down his features.

"What's wrong?" Steve asked.

"Oh," he said, "just finished a poker game over in the Union camp. Lost fifty bucks and some odd change. Last time I play with those blue-bellies. I'm going to bed."

Eventually, everyone else went to bed. I brought another chair a few feet away from Badger and sat down up-wind from him. The silence was thick between us. I didn't want to break it. I didn't want to start offering advice, analyzing his problems, trying to help him. I couldn't do that anymore. If I started talking, I might try, despite what happened two months ago. I wanted to know what was bothering him, what had made him go off with his old friends. He hadn't enjoyed his time with them. But I couldn't ask. I couldn't get involved in his problems. I would only make things worse.

I couldn't help him. I needed to go back to my tent, get some sleep before morning.

"Don't see why you guys would have anything to do with me," he said, his voice a low grumble.

I stopped before completely leaving my seat, then settled back down. "Well, you do smell pretty ripe, but we all need a shower."

He grunted, and it sounded a lot like a brief laugh.

Smoke from the dying fire blew into my face, and I stifled a gag. I coughed and tried to wave it off, but the breeze paid little attention to my protests.

"I messed up bad today," Badger said.

He wasn't drunk and I doubt he had had enough alcohol to make a man his size happy, let alone intoxicated.

"So you had a couple of beers," I said. "Big deal. You ran into some old friends and had some down time with them. So what?" I wasn't about to press him about his old acquaintances. They weren't your typical high school chums most people run across and have a quick chat about old times, but then Badger's past was not typical. Some of my former friends may have been questionable, but none of them were outlaw bikers.

"It ain't just that, Frank. I shouldn't have met up with Jewel and Red, not after all these years, not after ..." His words trailed off and he fell silent again, but I felt as though his brain was in full throttle, analyzing, searching for a way to continue. Finally, he said, "I guess you figured out my past ain't so perfect. I guess you guys knew I rode with a gang, but I bet you never knew the kind of crap we got into. I ain't proud of it, but it's done and gone. Drugs was a big thing. We used to sell the stuff, and I hate remembering that. It just turns my stomach to think about it. That bothers me worse than when we'd beat up people. Most of the time it would be rival bikers, or even street gangs wherever we might be, but sometimes just people who crossed us. Like the way you got into Diablo's face tonight. He was going to follow you out and get you in the parking lot, but I stopped him."

Visions flashed through my mind of possible scenarios of Diablo attacking me in the parking lot of Harley's. Instead of sitting here, sucking in acrid smoke, I could have been spending the evening in the emergency room with broken bones or stab wounds, sucking in oxygen through a hose in my nose; or worse, I could be lying on a slab in the morgue.

"Thanks," I told Badger with extreme sincerity.

"No problem." He looked over at me and grinned. "I told him you used to be a Navy Seal and you were a little nuts."

"Great." Maybe that might put Diablo off, but maybe it might make him curious, wondering if he could take on an ex-Seal.

He turned back to stare at the embers. "That bothers me, too. I lied. Ain't lied in a long time, and I don't like the taste it left. It's like this whole evening was just one big mess. You was there when I first saw Red and Jewel today. I didn't like seeing them, remembering what it was like back then. But then I started thinking about Jewel. You know, ten years ago she was hot, and we were an item. I really didn't want to see her again, but then we ran into each other again over by the sutlers. I think she was looking for me. Red wasn't with her, and she started in on how much she missed me, Red wasn't anything like me, we had great times. You know. I guess I got sucked into it, got tempted. Before I knew it, I was on the back of her Harley. We cruised around and, well, sort of started up where we left off. We ended up at that bar. Red got on her about me and her, but she put him down, and he just got stoned and drunk. And I kept hearing things about how times could be better now than they used to be. And all the while, I kept thinking about a verse from Second Corinthians by Paul, where he says 'Therefore, if any man be in Christ, he is a new creature: old things are passed away; behold, all things are become new.' But I'd keep arguing that my past hasn't gone away. Maybe I haven't changed. Maybe I'm still the same person. Maybe being born again doesn't work for people like me. I mean, I did some rotten stuff, Frank. I should have been in jail a dozen times. Came close enough, but I always got away. But I still think of all those things I've done. So when Jewel started hanging on me, I got to thinking maybe this is what I was meant to be, just an old biker. Nothing better."

"You can't believe that," I said, surprised that he'd even think it.

"Did you know I wanted to become a pastor? Yeah, I can't see it neither, now. I was working with the youth group at our church back home, and I thought maybe I could start a youth ministry, work with troubled kids. After all, they ain't done nothing worse than me. But I can't do it. Learned that tonight. I can't keep myself straight, so I sure as heck ain't going to tell kids what to do."

Actually, I couldn't see Badger as a minister. Even though he never lost his temper and until tonight I had never seen him mean, he just looked too big and intimidating. His smile cancelled all that and illuminated his gentle side, but he just did not have that outgoing demeanor of a preacher. Besides, "Pastor Badger" just didn't have a ring to it. I wasn't about to tell him my misgivings about his choices. But I also did not have any encouragement to offer.

"Why didn't you stay with Jewel, then?" I asked, suddenly afraid it might sound like a challenge. I actually just wanted to keep the conversation going in order to bring him out of his depression. I wasn't about to start offering advice.

"You," he said. "What you said."

I tried to remember what I might have said, and I couldn't recall coming up with anything very profound. I was angry at the time, and scared half to death, and now I couldn't think of anything I had said. The whole scene was just a blur. He must have seen my puzzled look in the faint glow of the dying fire.

"You asked me if that was what I wanted. And you said you guys were my friends. So I started thinking. And when I looked around at the pile of drunks and dope heads in that place, I realized I didn't want that. I didn't even want Jewel. Hey, I ain't no Einstein, but how long can I carry on a conversation with someone when the subjects are just hogs and drugs? And their friendship was never unconditional. They always wanted something. You guys don't. Neither does my pastor, come to think of it. Besides, I don't think I like beer anymore." He shoved his fist into his solar plexus and erupted with a burp that measured on the Richter. "I think it gives me heartburn."

"So you're not going to ride off on your hog?" I asked.

He chuckled. "Nah. You guys are stuck with me. I'm just sorry I put you through that. You risked a lot going into that place."

I shrugged. "Hey, that's what Navy Seals do."

He didn't laugh. "I treated you rotten. Sorry, Frank, but I didn't think I should be around you guys. I thought I belonged there, with the likes of Red and Diablo."

"You don't belong there anymore, Badger. You can't get rid of the past, but you can at least get rid of its influence." That sounded too much like advice. I slapped my knees and pushed myself up before I got carried away. "Hey, we'd better get some sleep. It's pretty late."

Chapter Seven

My heart is sore pained within me: and the terrors of death are fallen upon me ... Psalms 55:4

Malcolm Merryweather's house was not as large and grandiose as the Ramsey estate, but I could still put my own house in the living room and have plenty of space to walk around it. That's the difference between a teacher's salary and that of a banker. I was happy that Steve and I had cleaned up as best we could, in the limited privacy between the

"You. What you said."

rows of tents, and then dressed in our twenty-first-century civvies. Still, faded jeans, a wrinkled khaki shirt and an unshaven face did not fit these surroundings. Steve's tee shirt bearing the Confederate battle flag and a portrait of General Lee was a big hit with our host. Jake had not been thrilled with my decision to avoid the noontime battle, but I explained that I was in no mood to experience another temporal distortion on the field, right in front of the spectators. Considering the events of Friday, Jake saw the logic in that and dropped his argument. He passed me an annoyed look when I let him know that Steve was going with me to Merryweather's. When he saw us in our modern garb, he mumbled something about shooting us for desertion.

I had expected a gloomy house when I considered Merryweather's fascination with ghosts, but the home was filled with bright sunlight and warm furnishings. The paintings decorating the expansive living room were of peaceful landscapes. The mantelpiece held dozens of framed photographs of family members. Miranda apparently had siblings. There was a photo of a young man in an army dress uniform, then one of him in desert fatigues in some Middle Eastern wasteland. There was an older woman with Miranda's features with two young girls and a boy. She was absent in later photographs, though Malcolm was shown to age gracefully until he appeared in his present state. He was a distinguished man, usually wearing a tailored suit. Today, he wore slacks and a Polo shirt that probably cost more than I made in a week. Even casually dressed, he appeared crisp and in control. He made me feel as though I had come crawling for a loan and expected to be immediately turned down.

Yet he was the perfect host.

We had arrived with Miranda and her daughter, and he had met us at the door. He took us into the living room. In moments, a chubby middle-aged woman carried in a tray with tall glasses of iced tea, the glasses covered with condensation despite the cool climate provided by the home's air conditioning. Wedges of lemons floated beside the ice cubes.

"Come with me, Frank," Merryweather said after a volley of small talk.

He led me through a wide hall to a paneled door. The others followed in our wake. He grinned excitedly, like a boy showing off his latest toy, and pushed open the door.

Inside was a den with dark wood paneling, furnished with a huge oak desk that looked as though it had been carried here by the settlers of Jamestown. A corroded mortar shell served either as an oversized paperweight or a decoration. It was difficult to tell since there were no papers on the top of the desk. The keyboard and flat-screen monitor on the left side of the desk clashed with the surroundings. Sunlight flooded through high windows that were bordered by floor to ceiling bookshelves. The shelves were covered with volumes that ranged in age from old hardcover relics to modern paperback, dominated with subjects dealing in Civil War history. Some shelves were dedicated to books with titles similar to those I had seen for sale in his daughter's tent, with variations on the ghost theme. However, there were some with obscure titles that dealt with the darker side of the supernatural and the occult, which left me uncomfortable. Amidst the books, a decorative wooden box sat. The other walls were covered with swords, rifles, pistols, bayonets, knives and any other sort of weapon. A tattered Third National Confederate flag hung framed directly across from the desk, opposite the tall windows. The fabric of the flag had been torn and perforated with bullet holes. All sorts of paintings hung in frames, all depicting Confederate leaders in battle scenes or portraits.

A few squat leather chairs were scattered about, and the only other furnishing was a large table covered with an uneven topography mimicking fields and hills with miniature trees and shrubs. Regiments of two-inch high soldiers stood frozen in ranks that faced off blue against gray.

The room was a shrine to the Civil War.

For an excruciating half hour, Merryweather took me around the room and elaborated on almost every single item. Here was a saber found buried in a cornfield in West Virginia. There a collection of bullets he unearthed in the Wilderness. That carbine had been carried by an officer under J.E.B. Stuart. This saber had belonged to a general from Florida. That Navy Colt had seen service in Gettysburg. And so on.

At the table covered with topographical scenery in miniature, he described the conflict of the Battle of First Manassas represented by the little resin soldiers. He pointed out the little stream of Bull Run and told me how he hand painted each figure and built the scenery from scratch. On a slope sat civilians enjoying a picnic while watching the battle. He used a telescoping pointer to show me which miniatures represented which generals.

"There stands Jackson like a stone wall," he said, grinning, as the point of his wand hovered over a mounted figure with a thick beard.

He went through a monologue of the movements of the troops during the battle and took great pleasure at describing how the Union troops ran back to Washington. I nodded politely throughout the ordeal.

Like most people, Merryweather was under the impression that anyone participating in reenacting the Civil War was interested in all aspects of that period in history. I'm sure for the most part that is true. Reenactors are basically historians that try to bring that period of time alive. Some are military enthusiasts. I, however, was neither, and in my case Merryweather was under a false assumption. I was primarily a biologist, and if he wanted to discuss animal surgeries, ecological disasters, barrier reefs, or snake bites, I would have been thrilled. But his interests, outside of banking, were firmly rooted between 1860 and 1864. I was here because of Steve, and he had deserted me in favor of a tour of the grounds with Jenna. Miranda had also left, to give the housekeeper a hand with preparing lunch.

"I understand your group reenacts as a company that had started locally," he said eventually. "There were a couple of companies that began locally. You're with what company?"

"Huh?" I said, my brain numb. "Oh." I told him the name of the company and who had been the original commander.

He raised his eyes toward the ceiling. "Ah, yes, Captain Howard Long. Ramsey's Raiders. Tragic story. I wrote an article about the event for the magazine *Civil War Days*. I've written a number of articles over the years. I'd like to do a book some day, but I can never decide which subject to concentrate on. Maybe Ramsey's contribution to the war. I've done extensive research using letters and journals from local people of the time. That's how I pieced together the incident of the infamous train raid. There was never any official documents, since no one was ever charged."

He went to his bookshelves and took down the wooden box. After setting it on the desk, he lifted the lid. Inside were stacks of old papers sealed between plastic sheets. Beneath them at least two old leather-bound books peeked out. He lifted one sheet for me to see. It was a handwritten letter, the ink faded so much that it was difficult to make out the individual letters. The name scrawled at the top looked like Elijah Merryweather.

"This was from my great-great grandfather," he said, beaming. "I also have some of his private journals and correspondence. He was a colonel during the latter part of the war, though he was not involved in any battles. Started out as a simple merchant, became a local politician after the war, even started the bank I now manage. Material like this is invaluable to scholars and historians, even amateurs like me."

He replaced the sealed letter, lowered the lid and slid the box back into its place on the shelf. He treated the box as though it had been unearthed at Qumran and contained ancient scrolls. I related these old letters to discovering fossils, but beyond that I wasn't very impressed.

The scent of roasting herbs floated into the room and my stomach answered with a rumble.

"Finding these letters was like uncovering a gold mine," he said. "My articles barely scratched the surface."

"Then you probably have enough material to do a book," I said. I was more interested in the origin of the smells filling the house than I was in his research.

"Yes, I must say that I do. I simply need to organize it all and piece it together with the actual historical events that paralleled them. The journals are more illuminating. They provide great detail into the person's thoughts, though some entries are as vague as 'Today it rained'."

"How long ago was this article you did on the train raid?" I asked. Images of what I had seen the day before, or thought I saw, flashed through my mind and I thought of what Miranda and Jake had told me of the event. Maybe I had read his article or Steve had told me about it, or heard about it around the campfire on previous reenactments. Some previous exposure to the story would have contributed to my imagination, causing me to hallucinate in detail.

"About two years ago." He turned again to the shelf behind him and this time withdrew a slender magazine with a glossy cover depicting a raging Civil War battle, combatants frozen in the heat of the fight. He laid it carefully on the desk and opened it to an article entitled *The Forgotten Raid*. It bore his byline and was illustrated with an ink drawing of a shootout beside a train. It wasn't much like the vision I had experienced. My hallucination was more elaborate and more realistic. There were more Confederates involved in the illustration, about ten men shooting down five Union soldiers. And none of them used breech loaders. The strongbox was much larger, almost resembling a pirate's treasure chest. If my imagination had taken images from somewhere, it wasn't from this artist's rendition of the event.

"I'd like to read this," I said, and wondered why. Did I want to fan my own curiosity? Or did I want to convince myself that my hallucination was nothing more than my short-circuited brain's fantasy?

"Of course. But if you don't mind I'll find a copy on my computer and print it out for you. I only have a couple of copies of the magazine left, and I don't know if I can get any more back issues."

"That would be better. Thanks."

*****

After a lunch of grilled chicken, we retired to the living room to enjoy the air conditioning.

"Normally we would dine on the patio," Merryweather said, "but the heat is rather deplorable today. I'm certain you would prefer to be inside for a change. At least you should be a bit more comfortable without your wool uniforms."

I agreed with him.

"My daughter has told me about your experiences yesterday. Quite exciting."

I shook my head. I had hoped to avoid this discussion. The meal was great, but hardly worth my humiliation.

"To think," he went on with a wistful look on his face, "you had met Rebecca Ramsey the moment I was out on the patio listening to music. Had I known ... But I understand that you do not believe in ghosts. Do you still feel that way, even after last night?"

"Why would that change my mind? Mr. Merryweather—"

"Malcolm."

"Malcolm, I'm a scientist."

"I thought you were a teacher."

I hated when the conversation came to that. Every time, the same thing. A science teacher can't be considered a scientist. A science professor at some university, yes, but not a high school teacher. I had a degree in biology. I used to do research for a large company. Now I taught high school science. Did that change my training? Did that stop me from being a scientist?

"Dad used to do research," Steve put in. "Now he teaches."

"An admirable profession, Frank," Merryweather said. "And I suppose you contradict the old adage: Those who can, do; those who can't, teach."

"I've done it, now I teach it." I didn't bother to tell him that I would not be teaching long, that I would soon return to research. I knew that would involve relocating, but we would adapt. "But I'm still a scientist. I won't believe in ghosts because there's no evidence for them."

"But your own sightings ..." Merryweather protested.

I shook my head. "They can be explained in other ways. First of all, no one else saw the regiment of Union soldiers on the field. That was obviously caused by the heat affecting me. I was the only one who saw them, so I hallucinated. As far as Mrs. Ramsey in the mansion last night, I may have been the only one who saw her and so hallucinated that too, or she might have been someone dressed up to look like the late Mrs. Ramsey. Just about everyone there was in costume. We saw General Lee, President Davis, and a score of other famous people, but we never thought any of them were ghosts. Since it was evening, and a degree or two cooler, I might rule out the effects of the heat, so someone doing an impression is more likely."

"I asked around," Miranda said, "when your charming captain went with us into the mansion. No one saw a woman dressed like that, and none of the staff has ever hired anyone to dress up like Rebecca Ramsey."

I shrugged. No matter what I said, they wouldn't change their minds.

Merryweather tapped his index finger against his pursed lips. "Let me ask you this, Frank. Was Mrs. Ramsey wearing a light blue dress with a high collar?"

I nodded slowly.

"And did you happen to smell a fragrance, like a flowery perfume?"

"Lilacs," I said.

Now he nodded. "You see, Frank, I also saw her. Not last night, though, I'm sorry to say. But I have seen her a few times over the years. I often spend time at Ramsey House, going through their records and documents for my research. Most often she has been in the garden in early evening. Once, I entered the hall from the library and thought I was about to run right into someone. I stopped suddenly so we wouldn't collide, but there was no one there. And I often felt as though someone was looking over my shoulder as I studied old books or documents in the library or sitting room. Of course no one was there, but I always smelled the hint of perfume."

He could be making all that up, or he could be as crazy as me. Or more so.

"That's ... interesting," I said.

"But she actually spoke to you, didn't she?" he said in excitement. "You were right in front of her and she spoke. That is amazing! What was it she said? Someone was waiting for you? Who?"

I wanted to lie, just to stop this conversation and make more pleasant talk, but I couldn't. I could ignore certain questions, sidetrack answers, and even mislead. But I couldn't outright lie. Besides, Jake had told Miranda about the stranger in the crowd. "There was a man in the garden, dressed in a Union uniform."

"Did you know him?" Merryweather asked.

"I'd seen him before. And I spoke with him last night. He said my company was responsible for the murdered soldiers in that train raid you mentioned earlier. The one in your article."

Merryweather's face drained of color. He sat staring at me for so long that I had the urge to turn to look over my shoulder to see if some ghost had suddenly appeared behind me. I didn't turn, even though a chill curled up my spine. "He was probably someone playing a joke," I said. "Someone doing a Union colonel impression and getting carried away."

"But he specified the train raid. And your company."

"Yes."

He raked his fingers through his beard. "That was a terrible event. Not so much as other tragedies during the war, mind you. There had been so many atrocities and cruelties. This was minor compared to the whole war, which is probably why it was all but lost in obscurity. But those Union men were murdered and the money stolen. Captain Long and his men were responsible and should have been put on trial. In that box I showed you I have letters from some local figures concerning the event and proclaiming their guilt. If they had survived, they would have been brought up on charges. There were many letters from the families of the murdered soldiers demanding retribution and punishment. Maybe that's what your ghost colonel meant."

"That's only considering if the man was a ghost," I said. "Which he wasn't. Jake—our captain, Jake Boden—also saw him."

"I understand your son has some theory that does not include the supernatural," Merryweather said.

On the sofa next to Jenna, Steve perked up. "Ah, yes sir. Well, it's not my theory. I've read about, saw some documentary on it. It makes sense, since I don't believe in ghosts either."

"Oh, really." The corner of Merryweather's mouth curled up in amusement. His face had regained some of its color and he seemed more comfortable with the conversation, more in control. "So you don't believe in the supernatural?"

"Actually, I do. I believe in God, and He's supernatural. What I don't believe is a dead person's spirit floating around and making occasional appearances. What people may see is actually a temporal distortion that allows an image from another time to appear in our present, maybe interact with us. It's a matter of quantum physics." He explained the TV analogy, rambling on for some minutes, though Merryweather did not seem convinced.

"That's a good theory," he conceded, "but you won't mind if I reserve judgment on it. There are just too many strange things that your quantums can't explain. I can more easily believe in a person's spirit staying earthbound, especially when something is unresolved, as with our poor Rebecca Ramsey. After all, the human spirit is extremely powerful. It has the energy to remain here, pay us some visits or play some mischief. I'll take the spirit over your quantums any time."

"Well," I said, trying to bring this conversation to a close, "as you said, there are a lot of strange things in this world, too many to be explained with what little we know right now."

"But you won't believe in ghosts," he insisted. "You'd rather believe in a temporal quantum theory, even though there is probably less evidence for that."

"I'd feel more comfortable with it," I admitted. "At least it's an alternative to hallucinating."

"You would rather believe you hallucinated than believe in ghosts. I find that interesting. You are very prejudiced concerning the spirit world."

"Some things just do not fit into my personal idea of reality," I said.

"Ah yes, the scientist in you once more." He stroked his beard again. "You left research, you say. Any particular reason?"

"I wanted a less stressful job," I said, deadpan.

His brow rose up as the joke sank in.

"Cutbacks and downsizing," I said. "I thought it was time for a career change." And now it was time for another change, maybe back into research.

"And now you teach in a high school in Pennsylvania. Which one?"

"Pennswood."

His eyes lit with recognition of the name. "Ah, that one. It has been in the news recently, a couple of months ago. I'm so sorry. That was a tragedy."

"Yes," I said flatly, "it was."

I noticed Miranda's look of puzzlement, which flashed between her father and me, but I would not elaborate and her father chose not to go into details. They might do so later, him reminding her of the news reports from two months back. But he was too polite to talk about it in my presence. I could have told him there was a ghost in my life, one that haunted me every moment, especially in my dreams.

*****

I turned the truck over to Steve after returning to the battlefield. He and Jenna drove off to town to see some of the local sights, while I trudged across the field toward camp. The noontime battle still waged, the barking of muskets and the distant thunder of cannon rolling over the breeze. Cars filled the designated parking area and lined the highway. Spectators crowded over the hilltop that overlooked the fields between the Union and Confederate camps. The few bleachers that had been borrowed for the event were inadequate for the numbers. Many people had brought their own folding chairs, though most stood, sometimes on the tips of their toes to get as good a view as possible.

The camps were not deserted. Women either lounged in the shade of flies or busied themselves with chores around their camps. Children played and ran wild.

In our own camp, Doc chewed on the end of a cigar as he set surgical instruments out on a folding table. His white apron liberally stained with blood hung on a tent post. I walked up and looked over the array of instruments. I had seen them before many times, but I liked to examine them. Some resembled surgical instruments I had used both in graduate studies and in my research days. I knew that most were replicas, but some were prized originals, like the antique amputation saw, a couple of scalpels, a forceps, and a bullet extractor. When Doc is really enthusiastic, he piles up arms and legs made of latex and covered with the same artificial blood that stains his apron. There were no amputated limbs lying about, but Doc came out of his tent carrying an enamel pan with a discolored sponge floating in the crimson water.

"So, don't you know they shoot deserters around here?" he said. He set the bowl next to his instruments, wiped his hands on a white towel, then dropped the red-streaked cloth on the table for added effect.

"I figured I'd slip back into uniform before anyone got back," I said. "Maybe I could lay down on your stretcher and you can cut off an arm or a leg, just for emphasis."

He wagged a finger at me. "Now there's an idea. You change, I'll sharpen my saw."

I did change, but when I came out of my tent, Doc was lounging under the fly. The tin mucket in his hand glistened with condensation. He leaned back and flipped open the lid of the wooden ammunition crate sitting next to him. A cool mist rose up from the insulated interior of the crate, from the cans nestled in the bed of ice. Instead of ammunition, we carried ice and beverages, disguised against the passing tourists.

"Soda?" he asked.

I took a can, popped the lid, then poured the soda into my own tin cup.

I stashed the can into the plastic garbage bag hidden inside a canvas sack.

"What about that boy of yours?" Doc said. "Is he still AWOL?"

"He wanted to spend some time with his new friend and see the sights of greater Ramsey."

"Well, at least she's a southern girl."

"She lives in Pennsylvania with her dad. Her mother's from here."

"Close enough. Besides, we live in Pennsylvania, too." He thumbed open the lid on his mucket and took a drink. "Heard about your little adventure last night."

"In the biker bar? How's Badger doing today? I wanted to talk to him earlier, but we never got the chance to connect."

"He's on the field. He's a little more sullen than usual. But that's not what I was talking about. You had a visit with Mrs. Ramsey last night."

I wondered if the whole of the Confederate forces was aware of that particular event. Probably the Union forces as well.

"It's debatable."

"Still think you're going crazy?"

"More than ever."

"You don't sound very convincing. Come on, now, Frank. You're wondering if that was a real live ghost."

"Not a very accurate description. Isn't that a contradiction in terms? But, no, I know it wasn't a ghost."

"Well, it's just that first you saw that phantom regiment, then the lady of the manor. And some Union officer who is in question. It's getting to be a bit redundant."

"Well," I said, pinching my face in mock pain. "Actually, the soldiers on the field weren't the first." Then I went through the events of the train raid and the mysterious colonel. I finished up with the colonel's appearance at the Ramsey Mansion the night before. For a long time he sat and sipped his soda.

"That's a bit more complicated than just seeing one vision," he said eventually. "Now, with this thing involving that hundred and fifty year old train raid, it doesn't sound as simple as you going crazy. Seeing things is one thing, but coming up with a whole cast of characters is another. Do you still think you're hallucinating all this?"

I waved my arms, clanging the lid on my mucket. "I don't know. I can't see any other alternative."

"Maybe you should start believing in ghosts and save your sanity," Doc suggested.

"If I believed in ghosts, then the first one I'd see would be that boy," I said. I saw him in my dreams. I saw him if I shut my eyes in the middle of the day. If anyone would haunt me, he would. After all, I was the last person he saw, the last one he blamed. But I didn't see his ghost walking around. He haunted me in a different way.

Doc leaned closer. "Now look, Frank. That wasn't your fault."

"You weren't there," I snapped accusingly and immediately regretted my tone.

"No," he said, moving back, and his face sagged with old memories, "but I've been there. I've seen it in 'Nam and here. It ain't pretty, but it was never my fault. I've had to kill, but that was war. And they haunt me, too, Frank. Every one of them. I see my friends who died. I see the faces of the enemy I've killed. I can even imagine the ones I've killed from a distance. And I see the people who died when I was trying to save their lives. I see them all. I've learned to live with them."

"They never go away, do they, Doc?" I said, feeling the hopelessness.

A bugle sounded in the distance. The gunfire stopped and a cheer went up. The battle was over and the survivors and casualties would soon be wandering back into camp.

"You know," Doc said, his eyes looking out through the tents as though he could see the battleground, "I'd like to do one more battle. Side by side with my buddies. That was the best part about 'Nam, the guys. In minutes you made friends for life. In another minute they'd be gone forever. Here, we pretend. There isn't the danger, the threat. Except ... I have a threat hanging over me. The old ticker may not take it. In 'Nam, I didn't even think about dying. Heck, a nineteen-year-old is indestructible, right? But now, it's all I think about. And I don't mind telling you, it scares me." He spun on me and stabbed his finger at me. "But don't you dare say a word about that to anyone."

"About what?" I asked, giving him an innocent blank stare.

He grinned at me, but the smile faded fast. "I don't want to die, Frank."

"It helps," I said, "if you know where you're going after this life, if you have assurance. I want to go to heaven some day, just not today."

He chuckled.

Then we heard Jack, Badger, Daniel, Sam and Charlie singing "The Minstrel Boy" as they marched into camp.

Chapter Eight

I applied mine heart to know, and to search, and to seek out wisdom, and the reason of things, and to know the wickedness of folly, even of foolishness and madness ... Ecclesiastes 7:25

"That was your school?" Jenna asked.

She and Steve spoke in hushed tones at a back table in the small Ramsey Public Library. Considering the streets were filled with vendors of all sorts who were taking advantage of the weekend activities, the library was all but deserted. The lobby had displays of Ramsey's past, which brought a few of the curious inside, but most came in to enjoy a brief respite from the heat, take a quick browse, then venture out once more.

"Yep," Steve said.

"I remember seeing that on the news. They must have run the story for a week. Besides, you're not that far from where I live. Our football teams play each year. That was big enough news just locally, but it was all over the network news, too."

"Yeah. We finally get nationwide notoriety, and it had to be something like that. But it could have been worse."

"Did you know the kid?"

Steve shook his head. "Just to see him. We were in a couple classes now and then, and he would have graduated this year, too. Jeremy wasn't very sociable, didn't have many friends, didn't go in for sports or activities. But no one thought he was dangerous. He wasn't one of those guys that dress in black and wear swastikas. No one paid much attention to him, but he wasn't the only one. He wasn't a geek and I don't think he got picked on that much. There were other guys there that you'd expect to do something like that. I'm not the most popular guy in school either. I've been picked on, but I never thought to bring a gun to school and ..."

"You're not a geek."

"Tell that to the football team." He flashed a crooked grin but felt his face flush from what he took as a compliment.

"The news said he was going to shoot some other kids or some teachers," she said, her own cheeks coloring slightly. Her eyes moved away from his. "They were just spinning speculation, I guess, filling in time to keep the story going. Was he really planning to kill other kids?"

Steve shrugged. "I don't know. That's all we talked about the last two weeks of school. No one got much work done. The teachers weren't even into it. There were counselors there, y'know, in case someone couldn't cope. The buzz around the school was that he was going to kill a couple of the guys who teased him, then shoot himself. Most of the guys thought he was going to shoot the teachers that flunked him and kept him from graduating. No one knows. He didn't talk much. But we're pretty sure someone else would have been dead if things didn't go the way they did."

Jenna became very quiet. "That was your dad, wasn't it?"

"Yeah. He was there."

"I remember seeing him on the news. He looked pretty shook up."

"Yeah. That was him."

Steve didn't speak for a while, just stared at his hands in front of him. Jenna reached over and laid her hands softly over both of his.

"What happened?" she asked.

"Dad won't talk about it. It was during homeroom, and one of his kids had seen Jeremy's gun. It was an automatic, a 9mm. I think. He had it shoved in his belt, hidden under his shirt. This guy who saw it came into my Dad's room and started telling everyone. Dad went to find Jeremy to see what was going on. He saw him slip into the restroom and followed him. Dad tried to talk Jeremy into handing over the gun, but it didn't work. One of my friends was in Dad's homeroom. They overheard some of it while other kids went for help. I was in my homeroom down the hall. We all heard the gun go off. I think the whole school did. At least he kept Jeremy in the restroom. It was all over by the time the police got there."

"Oh my God," she said, barely audible. "He could have shot your dad."

"Yeah, I know. He wasn't in Dad's class, so Dad wasn't one of the teachers who were failing him. But if he got upset enough, he could have shot him. I don't think my Dad thought of that, though. That's not what's bothering him."

"What, you think Jeremy dying upset your dad?"

"Well, it's not every day some guy blows his brains out in front of you."

Jenna stared down at her hands entwined in Steve's. "So ... maybe he has been seeing things. Because of what happened."

Steve squeezed her fingers. "I think he thinks that."

She looked hard into his eyes. "But you don't think it's ghosts, do you?"

"Nope. It's not ghosts. When you die you either go to heaven or hell. But something weird is going on. I don't know what it is. I think the more we know, the better we can help. It all comes down to that train raid when the Union soldiers were killed and the money stolen. He said that Union colonel wanted revenge for that. I know it doesn't make much sense, but maybe we can figure something out."

She grinned. "And that's why we're here, huh?"

"Yep. We've got to find out what the library has on that raid, or Captain Long's command. There might be some articles, maybe some old newspapers. Then we can check the Internet."

"What about the letters and stuff my grandfather has?"

Steve and Jenna moved to a table that had a computer with the library catalog already activated. He began typing in some key words.

"If we don't find much, that's an option," he said.

"Don't you have a battle to go to?"

"Probably already missed it. Besides, I'd rather be here." He didn't add that it didn't matter whether they were in the library or not, but from the expression on her face she knew that.

There was actually very little on that particular train raid. There were no books that referred to it and no articles in any magazines presently kept in the library. The local paper, the *Ramsey Times*, had undergone many changes, particularly owners and names. Issues were kept on microfiche. Even with the help of one librarian, it took time to get the filmstrips for the range of dates they wanted and to figure out how to use the viewer. Steve would have preferred using the computer for everything, but the newspaper issues just weren't available on the Net. He was very much aware of the warmth of Jenna's arm next to his as they sat close together in front of the viewer. She was, however, a distraction in his concentration of the newsprint that passed over the viewer screen. Good thing they were both scanning the same pages.

"What was that?" she asked.

"Huh?"

"Go back, go back. There! Stop."

He read, "September 21, 1861. Howard Long and his state militia, known as Ramsey's Raiders, leave to become part of the 13th Virginia Infantry." He scanned through the small article, then shook his head. "Doesn't say much, just that the militia was mustered in to became part of the regular army. Long was chosen to be captain because he had experience in the Mexican War. Long was a local farmer, it says."

Jenna's eyes roamed the image on the plastic screen. "Nothing about a train."

"No. And according to what I heard, the militia raided the trains now and then before becoming part of the regular army. So any raid would have occurred before September 21, 1861. This article doesn't say anything about trains."

He turned to see her rubbing her eyes. "Tired? We haven't found anything. Maybe we should give it a rest. At least take a break."

"Maybe we could try the Internet. It's been over an hour and a half and we haven't found anything."

"My dad says research takes time. He used to do research for a big company. But he tells me research papers in college are going to be pretty rough. It's not like high school."

"You start college in a few weeks, right?"

Steve frowned. "Yeah."

"You don't sound very excited about it. I've still got my senior year and I can't wait to get through it and go to college."

"It's a big change," he said.

"Change is good," she said brightly, trying to lighten his mood.

He shrugged, not convinced.

"Will any of your friends be going there?" she asked.

"A couple. It's not that far from us, but I'll still have to live on campus, commute home on weekends, if I can afford the gas."

"Actually, I applied there for next year. It's down the road from us, two towns over, about twenty miles, so I'd live off-campus. My dad wanted me to go to a bigger college, but I'm not that thrilled to move away. It's bad enough I leave home in the summer to come here. Of course, once I'm eighteen I won't have to do that. I love my mother and all, but she's a little strange."

"I hadn't noticed," Steve said, his gloom now dissipated.

Soft footsteps behind them stopped Steve from suggesting a walk through the town, along the short Main Street. They both turned toward the older librarian as she waddled toward them. Her glasses hung from a strap around her neck and bounced back and forth as she walked. Her nametag said "Mrs. Pennington."

"Now just what are you children trying to find? You've been at it for nearly two hours." He voice was light and friendly, thick with an accent from the deeper South.

"Ah, well," Steve began, "we're doing some research on the early part of the Civil War."

Her face soured. "You mean the War of Northern Aggression, child."

"We're looking for information on the train raids the local militia did

"Now, just what are you children trying to find?"

before they became part of the regular army," Jenna said, and Steve noticed that her accent had changed. She did a perfect imitation of her mother.

The librarian smiled.

"Child, that was miles from here, up north toward Maryland. Those trains carried supplies and Union troops to the west. And passengers, too."

"Then the local militia didn't raid the trains?" Steve asked, frowning. He wondered if all this was a waste of time and the raids never happened to begin with.

Her hand flew in a dismissive wave. "Of course. It was just a few days march north. But t'wasn't anything that local papers would cover at that time. At least I wouldn't think so. They'd march north, set a trap or board the train somehow, then rob it, and head south again before the troops would pick up their trail. Sometimes they'd just mess the track up so the train couldn't get through and pass on their supplies or troops. If there weren't too many soldiers on board, they'd rob it. Either steal money or the supplies, whichever they could carry. You know, dear, that was where the train robbers of the Old West learned their trade. They started out robbing the Union."

"Were there payroll shipments on those trains?" Steve asked.

"Every month or so, at least at the start of the war. Got to be few and far between later on. Those soldiers west had to get paid from Washington."

He looked over at Jenna and shrugged. "At least that all fits." Then he looked back at Mrs. Pennington. "You know a lot about this, don't you, ma'am?"

"Sure enough. I get an awful lot of time to read. But what you're asking, I got most of that from talking to the local ladies. I'm from South Carolina originally. But the ladies here just adopted me. We have tea at each other's houses every week, and we get to talking. Well, most of these ladies have had families here since the Indians were chased out, and they have so many stories. Now, mind you, I don't believe a word of half of it, but a few, like Margaret Letterman and Cynthia Reed, we call her Cyn, they have letters and papers from their ancestors, some dating to Revolutionary times. Margaret's the one who had something about the railroad. She was either related to one of those Confederate soldiers or her late husband was. Can't rightly remember which."

Steve and Jenna both glanced at each other.

"Can you give us …"

"Can we have her …"

The librarian waved her hand again. She reached into a little cardboard box sitting next to the fiche viewer and withdrew a scrap of paper and a pencil no longer than two inches. She bent down over the table to write on the paper. Her glasses dangled in the air and swayed as she wrote.

"Now, mind you she might not be home, but I'm sure she'd like a visit from you young people. And she does love to talk. Can't get a word in sometimes. Here's her address. And show her the note I put down with it, if the woman has her glasses on. It says I sent you. Now why don't you two get out of here and enjoy some of that beautiful sunshine out there?"

*****

Mrs. Letterman's house was a small ranch style with pale-blue siding and a small front yard bursting with flowers. A white picket fence no taller than two feet stopped the foliage from spilling out onto the sidewalk. In the deep shade of the front porch, a rocker creaked. Steve and Jenna stopped at the little gate and double-checked the address on the scrap of paper, then looked at the figure rocking in the shadows. Ice tinkled in a glass.

"Well," said a sharp voice, "don't just stand there, come inside and speak your mind. You aren't selling magazines or something, are you? Not one of those ghost hunters, eh? No, too early for that. None of them don't seem to realize this house ain't more than fifty years old. Used to be a pasture right under here, so they're welcome to come if they want to see a ghost cow or goat. Well, speak up, you two."

"Mrs. Letterman?" Jenna asked hesitantly. She still used the southern accent, mimicking her mother. Steve guessed it would put the local people more at ease than if she sounded like she actually came from Pennsylvania or some other northern state.

"Sure enough. And you? Don't stand out there, come up here. I don't like talking long distance without a phone. Now what's your name, young lady?"

"I'm Jenna Connor and this is Steve Blaine. The librarian, Mrs. Pennington, suggested we pay you a visit."

"Ruby? Bless her soul."

As Steve and Jenna climbed onto the porch and came into the cooling shade, Jenna held out the note the librarian had written. Margaret Letterman was thin and straight, wearing jeans and a polo shirt, both marked with dirt stains, particularly on the knees. Her sneakers had once been white Nikes but were now covered with dirt and grass stains. Her bright blue eyes flashed between the two teenagers and belied her seventy years. Her hand steadily held a glass of iced tea, condensation dripping from its surface to make a little puddle on her lap.

She took the note and glanced at it, her eyes squinting. "Can't never make out her scribbling. Dear ol' Ruby must not have been wearing her glasses. Can't make this out very well. Makes no never mind. What brings you two out here on such a nice day? Me, I just got finished doing some gardening. Care to join me for some tea? You, young lady, go inside. It's all right. Just go into the kitchen, get two glasses. The tea's in the refrigerator in a pitcher, ice in the freezer where it should be. Pour you and your young gentleman friend a nice tall glass, then join me here."

She motioned to the assortment of wicker chairs surrounding her.

Steve felt uncomfortable sitting with the woman while Jenna went into the house. He heard cabinets opening and closing, ice clinking into glasses, then Jenna pushed her way out the screen door, a tall glass in each hand. She passed one to Steve as she sat down in the wicker chair next to him.

"Thanks," he said quietly. And then to the woman, "Thanks, Mrs. Letterman."

"Don't thank me till you taste it. Now, what brings you here? I'm not on the list of tourist sites, am I?"

"Mrs. Pennington told us you would know some facts about the Civil War," Jenna said. "We're researching the local militia and the train raids they used to do."

"Oh, Ramsey's Raiders, that's what they were. Yes, an ancestor of my late husband, Herbert. His great uncle was the captain of the group, I believe."

Steve's mouth dropped open. "Do you mean Howard Long?"

"Oh, my yes. That's him. We had a ton of letters from him to all different members of his family, and all sorts of documents. Even had the letter informing his family of his death. Poor man was killed by friendly fire, just like dear Stonewall Jackson. Happened far too often, back then. Herbert held onto all of that. He also had other ancestors in the war, so he had a mess of papers. I had a few on my side, but not much ever came down through the family to my generation. Howard Long, though, owned quite a bit of farmland. Too bad that never made it this far. His family lost it not long after he died, or else Herbert might have been a wealthy landowner. But I'm satisfied with what we had. We had a good life."

"Do you know anything about a train raid when Union soldiers were murdered?" Steve asked, leaning forward in his chair, causing the wicker to squeak.

"Now, a lot of soldiers died. Those weren't pleasant times, son."

"No, I mean that the soldiers on the train surrendered, but they were killed anyway. Murdered, not killed in battle."

She shrugged. "A lot of that happened on both sides, dear. Now, I don't recall anything particular with Howard Long's unit."

Jenna said, "There was a rumor that his men robbed a train, murdered the soldiers and kept the money. Anything like that?"

She laughed. "If he had, there must not have been enough money to go around. His property was sold off for debts after he died, bought up by some local merchant. That's why his descendants never had a clog of it. Too bad you couldn't look in his journal. Never read it myself, but it might tell you something."

"You have his journal?" Steve almost slipped from the chair.

Jenna's hand on his arm stopped him from jumping up in excitement.

"Did. Most of the papers were donated to museums, a couple were sold to collectors. Do you know what someone paid for that letter to his family about his death? It had General Johnson's signature on it. We had quite a vacation that year. But that journal. It was here until recently. That banker from town borrowed it for his own research. He's a history buff, too, and said he was writing a book or something about the local people in the war. He offered me some money for it, but I wanted to keep it and pass it on. He promised to give it back, even wrote out an agreement that he was only borrowing it. I wonder if he's finished with it."

Steve glanced at Jenna. She was leaning forward now, her eyes round and expectant. Her mouth formed on O before she spoke. "Who borrowed the journal?"

"Why, Mr. Merryweather, from the bank."

"That's my grandfather."

Mrs. Letterman grinned. "What a small world, dear. Maybe you can ask him about it. I'd like to have it back, not that it's worth much, but it belonged to Herbert. I'd like to pass it on to our children. Well, maybe the grandchildren. Our sons aren't very interested, which is why we've kept all the papers here, and sold or donated the others. But maybe the grandchildren would like to know something of their ancestry. They seem a bit more interested in history than our two boys ever were."

"That's a good idea, Mrs. Letterman," Jenna said. "I'll see if I can get it from my grandfather and get it back to you."

"Thanks, dear. I still have that agreement he signed. See if he wants that back. Won't do me any good once I have the journal back. Now, how about some more tea?"

*****

At the door to Malcolm Merryweather's house, the housekeeper shook her head. "I'm sorry, dear, but your grandfather is out. He was wearing that general's uniform, so I believe he went off to one of the functions for the Civil War reenactors. It might have been something at the Ramsey House again, but I'm sure I don't know. I haven't the vaguest idea when he'll be back."

"That's okay, Mrs. Banks," Jenna said. "We'll catch up with him."

"I was just on my way out myself," the woman said, "or you wouldn't have caught me. I need to pick up a few things for dinner tonight. I believe you and your mother will be joining us. Will your young friend be along?" she asked, smiling at Steve.

"Ah, no, I don't think so," Steve said. "I've got to get back to our camp."

"Well, there'll be plenty if you change your mind. That is, if I get to the store."

"Sorry to keep you, Mrs. Banks," Jenna said. "Bye."

She tugged on Steve's arm to get him to follow her off the porch and back to the truck."Why didn't you ask to see the papers?" He hissed at her in a whisper that wouldn't be caught by the housekeeper as she closed the front door.

"Because," Jenna said casually through a pleasant smile, "she wouldn't have let me. This isn't my house, and my grandfather is a bit protective of his den. It's like his own private museum. That place is out-of-bounds unless my grandfather is there. She would have stood her ground and insisted we wait for Granddad to come back. On a good day she might have offered us milk and cookies, but she still wouldn't have let us past the kitchen."

"So, we just give up?"

At the truck, she turned an exasperated look at him. "Oh ye of little faith."

He opened the passenger door for her, his face a maze of puzzlement. He climbed into the driver's side and wiggled his keys free from his jeans. He was beginning to understand what his father always said about women, particularly when his mother wasn't within earshot.

"Okay, now what?" he asked as he started the engine.

"Now, we wait for Mrs. Banks to go shopping. Drive down the block and park. We shouldn't be sitting out front."

They did not have long to wait. The housekeeper rolled out of the drive in her little Subaru and sped off in the opposite direction. Steve shifted the truck in gear, but Jenna stopped him, laying her hand over his on the shift.

"Maybe we should leave the truck here," she suggested.

"What, are we going to break in?"

"Technically, no. Come on."

She was a few paces down the sidewalk before he climbed out. He glanced around the neighborhood and was grateful that no one was out to witness their suspicious behavior. He imagined eyes behind curtains, watching their every move. He tried to act casual as he caught up to Jenna, but he knew he looked like some skulking thief about to plunder an empty house. The house would be surrounded with patrol cars before they got across the lawn.

In front of the porch, Jenna stepped into the garden and overturned a rock. Her fingers dug into the soft earth and withdrew a small plastic box. She popped this open and triumphantly held up a key.

"Mom had to use it a couple times when I was with her," she explained.

She brushed the dirt off her hands as she stepped up to the front door. She unlocked it, then trotted back down to the garden to replace the key.

Inside the hall, they both stopped to stare at the flashing lights of the security panel on the wall.

"Oh-oh," she said. "I forgot about that. I can't remember if Mom knew that code or not."

Steve wondered how much time they had before the alarm started ringing. Was it silent or would it wake the neighborhood as they conspicuously retreated back to the truck? Jenna stared at it, fingers flexing as though she could make them think of the code. Steve looked over her shoulder. How much time did they have before it went off? They should get out before ...

"Uhmm," he said, tapping her shoulder, then he pointed to the LED status on the panel. "It's inactive."

Jenna squinted at it. "Oh. Good. I guess Mrs. Banks didn't want to bother with it if she didn't expect to be gone for long. We'd better hurry."

They continued down the hall to the den. At least this door wasn't locked, although he wouldn't be surprised if Jenna whipped out a lock pick from the pocket of her jeans.

Steve took in the huge wooden desk, with its mortar shell paperweight and flat-screen computer monitor. Then he spun slowly to look at the decorations on the walls, the battle-worn Confederate flag in its frame, the paintings, the mounted weapons, the shelves of books, and the large table with its ranks of resin miniatures awaiting orders to advance into battle. Jenna hefted a wooden box from the shelf. She set it carefully on the desk and lifted the lid. Steve drew close, looking over her shoulder, smelling the fresh fragrance of her blond hair.

He shook himself and concentrated on the contents of the box.

The papers sealed in plastic were yellowed with age. The faded ink scrawls were hard to read, but he recognized some words at first glance. He thought he could read the name Elijah Merryweather, and the date was something, 1863. Probably from one of Jenna's ancestors.

"One of my ancestors owned a general store about that time," she said. "That might have been him, or one of his cousins. Might be the one my grandfather talks about, who became mayor of Ramsey after the war, started the bank he manages." She stacked the papers on the desk.

"There!" Steve said, reaching around her to jab a finger at a ragged leather book.

Jenna already had her fingers around the book. She stopped to look down at Steve's arm encircling her as he pointed needlessly at the journal. He quickly pulled his hand back, clasping both hands behind his back. He felt his face heat up.

She brought the book out and carefully lifted the cover. The spine cracked.

Steve's cheek brushed against Jenna's hair as he drew a little closer over her shoulder to see the first page.

"Elizabeth Merryweather," she said, reading the name on the title page. "Another ancestor."

Steve looked at her. "You think?"

She closed the journal and glared at him. "I've got all that stuff written down at home, our family's who's who. But nobody in our family ever did anything very interesting, so it gets a bit hard to remember everyone, especially when the names are similar."

Some more letters and documents were removed, and an old cloth-wrapped book lay exposed. Steve thought it better to remain silent and let Jenna deal with it. She unwrapped it, cradled the leather volume in her palm, opened the cover, and squinted at the faded ink.

"'1862, Howard Long, Thirteenth Virginia Volunteer Infantry,'" she read out loud. "This must be it."

She handed the journal to Steve, who opened it reverently while she replaced all the other papers. She closed the box and set it back on the shelf.

"What if this isn't the right journal?" he asked. "Could there be another one by Long?"

Jenna shook her head. "Mrs. Letterman only mentioned one, so that's it. Let's see what it says."

"Yeah. It might not have anything useful. Look at this entry—'Friday, it rained again.'"

"Well, skip that one. Let's just have a look." She took the book back and gingerly flipped through some pages. "All these dates are well after that train raid. By this time Long's part of the regular army. When did they muster in, September, 1861? We might have to read the whole thing to find anything worthwhile."

"Ah," Steve lifted his finger to cut her off. "I don't think we can do that here. I hear someone outside."

The front door opened.

Chapter Nine

And he said to them all, If any man will come after me, let him deny himself, and take up his cross daily, and follow me ... Luke 9:23

The battle raged ahead of us. Our lines, squeezed shoulder to shoulder, strung out over the crest of the hill. We marched down the gentle slope, accompanied by the roar of our cannon. The Union troops pushed back our first lines of attack, and we came in as reinforcements to flank them. Bodies in gray and butternut littered the field, accompanied by two or three in blue.

"Battalion ..." came the command from Colonel Wessner.

"Company ..." echoed the command from the company captains down the ranks.

"Ready, aim ..."

We cocked our hammers and lifted our muskets.

"Fire!"

The blast echoed across the hills. Once the ringing left my ears, I heard the spectators applauding.

Dozens of Union soldiers dropped now, and a few in our own ranks fell from the returning volley. Daniel grabbed his shoulder, spun like a ballet dancer, then dropped with an exaggerated grunt. The Federal troops withdrew under our assault as we advanced. We crested that hill, and were met by two dozen Zouaves in their fancy red trousers, short blue jackets, and red fezzes. They fired and charged at us. We stood our ground and returned fire.

The Zouaves halted, formed their lines, and fired at our advance. We lost more men, but we fired in return and then charged.

Our rebel yell was terrifying.

The Zouaves retreated, never losing a man.

I had decided to take an early hit, but I never had the opportunity. I only joined the battle under pressure from the rest of the company. Everyone believed I would be fine, that no more hallucinations would trouble me, that I was needed since Steve hadn't returned to camp by the time of muster. Besides, as Sam put it, what were the odds of more ghosts showing up in the middle of the day after yesterday's appearance? So I got my leathers, loaded my cartridge box, and pulled my musket free of its canvas cover. I joined the troops as we marched into battle at about three in the afternoon, and I wondered what sort of things I might imagine this time.

I went along mechanically, following everyone else, working on automatic, while my mind turned over the utter weirdness of this weekend. I hadn't hallucinated for two months since the shooting, so why now? Well, a weekend of reenacting has a sort of surreal sense about it. We were in a different time, or rather caught between two time periods. If you tried to rationalize it, it might drive you nuts. This was probably a perfect venue for my imagination to slip in and work overtime. I just needed a real vacation, some warm beach somewhere, lots of sunshine, and a new career to look forward to—a quiet lab somewhere where I could work on a cure for terminal insanity.

The Union troops had reformed and flanked us on the right. We wheeled in that direction, shot a few volleys, then made our own retreat.

We rallied at our colors behind a low wall of stone. Here we made a brief stand as the mass of Union soldiers advanced. We put up a brave fight and a good show, but we fell under the blue onslaught. I dropped over the wall, my arms dangling. Sam pirouetted, then fell on the other side, one leg hung over the stones. The casualties were abandoned as our comrades retreated and the Federals stormed the wall.

The bugle sounded the end of hostilities.

Cheers rang out and the spectators applauded.

I reached underneath me and pushed myself up from the stone wall. I had laid my musket against the stones and grabbed it as I stood up. I was about to lend a hand to Sam to help him up when I noticed that the man lying where Sam had fallen was in an entirely different position. He was sprawled on the ground in front of the wall, arms and legs akimbo. He was not short and stocky like Sam, either. This man was gaunt, as though starved from months of hardships. And this man was staring into the sky through milky eyes. A blackened hole pierced his forehead.

I heard the flies as though they were buzzing inside my ears, but they were swarming over the body and the black pool of blood that soaked into the ground underneath. Slowly I looked to either side of me. My fellow reenactors were nowhere to be seen. I was alone, or at least I was the only one standing.

The breeze tickled my skin and brought the stench of decay to my nostrils. I sucked in the putrid air, then held my breath. All around me lay the bodies. Some dressed in blue, some in gray, all tattered and worn and covered in filth. The gray uniforms were in worse condition. The faces were still thin even as the bodies began to bloat from the first stages of putrefaction.

Hundreds of bodies.

The sounds of battle were long gone, the smell of powder had dissipated. The only movement over the field were from the flies and the birds, come to scavenge.

I felt inclined to chase the birds away, to stop them from desecrating the dead, but this wasn't real. I was hallucinating. My imagination had gone into overdrive. Warp drive.

I turned very slowly. The dead lay all about me.

My knuckles whitened as my hands tightened around my musket. I took a few hesitant steps. I felt the uneven ground and the clumps of grass under my feet. Flies scattered at my movement, formed a dark buzzing cloud, and swarmed back over their victims.

"Sam?" I said, my weak voice lost in the vastness of the fields.

The call of a crow answered me. It flew down to provoke an argument with some of its cousins. They hopped around between the corpses, jabbing their beaks at each other like swordsmen dueling over a treasure.

I remembered Steve's theory of temporal distortions, how we saw things through a tear in time. He had explained my hallucinations that way, and had even suggested that the cold spot Jake and I encountered with Miranda Connor was the place where a distortion might be forming. I remembered now Jake's question of whether we could go through that rift into the past. Steve hadn't believed so. Now I wondered. I was either hallucinating to perfection and experiencing a massive nervous breakdown, or I just stepped into the past. My surroundings looked very much like the aftermath of the battle of Pine Creek.

I hadn't felt any cold spot, but I wasn't too concerned about details. What concerned me was how to get back. If I had indeed been transported to the past, how long would I stay there? I wasn't prepared to become a permanent resident of 1862, especially in the middle of a war, and I was dressed in the uniform of the side that lost. It might be interesting to talk with some famous historical figures, like those whose look-alikes were at the party at the Ramsey mansion last night. I even had the ability to alter history. I could change the outcome of the war, help Lee win at Gettysburg, change the course of history. I could bring about medical advancements decades before their times, save millions of lives. I could use my knowledge to become the richest man ever. And I would never see my family again.

I was definitely having a breakdown.

I wanted to call for my friends, but I was afraid someone might answer. Someone whom I didn't know. I might even be grateful for the appearance of the enigmatic Union colonel. No one showed up. If this were real, wouldn't burial details be coming through to take the bodies away? Medical people must have already been here, since there were no wounded visible or within the range of my hearing. What surrounded me was a vast graveyard where all the corpses lay on the surface.

How long had they been dead?

I bent down, using my musket like a staff to steady myself, and stared at the nearest man. The flies swarmed around the gaping hole in his chest. Blood stained the gray wool black. When I looked at his face, I saw that he was no more than a boy, probably younger than my son. Images of Jeremy Hicks flashed through my mind, that boy lying on the dirty tiles, his face distorted in the brief agony of death. This boy looked nothing like Jeremy. His filthy face was so thin he might not have eaten for months and had not washed in the same amount of time. He had probably been ill before being shot. One hand lay closed over his stomach, the other at his side. He may not have died instantly, but with that wound he would have had only moments, and he would have known he was going to die within a few minutes.

My hand slowly moved toward him. This couldn't be real, but the hallucination was so detailed. My fingers brushed the rough wool of his shell jacket. They pushed deeper, feeling the hardness of the forearm underneath.

The boy's arm slid down and I jumped back, almost stumbling over another body behind me. His arm fell to the ground and the closed hand opened. I saw a glint of silver in his palm.

I bent down again and looked. Something lay inside the curl of his relaxed hand. I couldn't bring myself to touch the body, so I tapped the hand with the butt of my musket. A small silver object tumbled to the ground. I reached over and picked it up. Standing, I turned it over in my fingers.

It was a small silver cross about an inch long. The ring on its end that would have held it to a chain was broken and gaping. The boy may have torn it off or he may have kept it in his pocket after it broke. He may have pulled it out when he lay dying, to comfort his last moments of life. The metal felt cold against my fingertips, but most importantly, it felt real. It wasn't very comforting to me.

"Find something?"

The sound of the voice next to me startled me so much that I jumped back, dropping my musket.

Sam started laughing, and I became aware of voices all around me. Men were discussing the battle, complaining about command, commenting on dinner. Some men stood in little groups, while most slowly wandered off toward their respective camps. Invitations were called out, promises shot back. All the casualties had risen and were once again alive and whole. No dead littered the field. What blood I saw was the red of theatrical blood staining cloths or faces for the benefit of the spectators. The ground was not stained. No swarms of flies attacked and no birds dueled for carrion. Sam bent down, picked up my musket by the barrel, and held it toward me. I stared at him. Was he an hallucination?

Taking the musket, I mumbled a thanks.

"What did you find?" he asked.

I opened my palm. The silver cross lay there. But the dead boy who had owned it was gone. Buried a hundred and fifty years ago.

*****

"Can you loan me a few bucks?" Sam asked as we walked back to camp.

My mind was still reeling from my trip into the past, pondering if I actually transported back and forth in a fraction of a second. Logically it was impossible. Time travel just didn't happen. At least it was more scientific than ghosts, but it was still impossible, at least with our present technology. That wasn't to say that a future generation couldn't develop time travel and travel back to our time. And with that path of reasoning, the weekend just became a lot more complicated. It was simpler to say that

I, once again, hallucinated. My brain had fried, my wiring short-circuited. I was a prime candidate for a room at the laughing academy. Reservations were already made.

Except for the silver cross medallion.

I kept it in my hand and opened my fingers to stare at it as we walked. I could not put it in my pocket, fearing that it would disappear, just like the corpse of the boy who had it. This was hardly proof that I time traveled. After all, according to Sam I had been next to him all the time. I hadn't vanished from view of anyone in the present, although I spent several minutes on the battlefield of the past. Had I thought of it, if the idea of proof had entered my mind, I could have rifled through the belongings of any one of the corpses for personal belongings, preferably something with a name and date. A newspaper would have been nice, or someone's personal journal. Some men carried metal disks that were the precursors of dog tags. One of those could have been useful. But this cross had no marking, no inscriptions. One of the reenactors could have lost it.

"Frank?" Sam said.

"Ah, what for, Sam?" I asked.

"There's a game going on in the Union camp, some Pennsylvania guys. I'm running a little short. But I know I can beat some of these guys."

"I thought you said you'd never play with Union men again," I reminded him.

"Yeah, well, these guys are amateurs. It'll be a piece of cake and I can humble a few Yankees while I win my money back. Pay you back as soon as the game is over."

I didn't like his gambling. None of us did. Some companies got a bad reputation for gambling or drinking, and we didn't care for the stigma. Most reenactors were family oriented. Besides, Sam's gambling had caused personal problems. Last year he lost his job for doing Internet gambling in the office. His wife had left him, temporarily, according to him. She'd just gone to Philly to visit her mother. Through the grapevine we learned it would be permanent if he didn't straighten up.

"Sorry, Sam," I said, "Steve has my wallet. It's locked in the glove box in the truck."

He pursed his lips, not saying anything, but not believing me. He wouldn't call me on it, for which I was grateful. True enough, my wallet was in the truck, but I also had money in my pocket. I hated deceiving him, but I also hated giving him money to lose in another card game. He knew my stand and didn't want to get into another disagreement.

"How's Ellie?" I asked.

"Huh? Oh, fine. Still out at her mother's. Her mother hasn't been too well. Ellie's still taking care of her. Might be a few more weeks."

"Is she important to you?" I asked.

"My mother-in-law?" he asked, incredulous.

"Ellie." I stopped and glared at him.

He stopped a step ahead, looked at me, then looked down at his worn brogans. "Well, yeah, of course."

"It all comes down to what's more important," I said. Then I walked away.

"Frank, Frank," he called after me, trotting to catch up. "I know, you're right. Hey, gambling is just for fun. I'm not addicted like those guys that run to Atlantic City every weekend or call a bookie all the time. Heck, I don't even know any bookies. I just like playing cards, dropping a few bucks on the lottery now and then. Well, okay, so I buy a few lottery tickets each week, but it's like an investment. Never know when one of those will pay off big. After all, somebody has to win, why not me? And it's not like I lose all the time. I'm pretty good at cards. I probably could give those Vegas people a run for their money. But I'm not addicted. I don't waste my whole paycheck. I pay my bills, and then I have some fun."

And his wife drives a twelve-year-old car that had to be towed more times than driven. She hasn't been on a vacation for five years except to an occasional reenactment. And according to Sarah, who is part of the grapevine among the reenactors' families, Ellie hasn't bought any new clothes in over two years. I didn't bother to enter into the argument. He's heard it all before.

"Sorry, Sam, I don't have anything to lend you." Still not technically lying. I had money, but it was not going to be lent out.

He waved a dismissive hand. "Forget about it. I'll skip the game this time."

He left me alone on our walk back to camp, and my mind spun over my recent experience that might be described as time travel. I wanted to talk this over with Steve, see if it fit in with his temporal theories. Most of all, I just wanted to see him, make sure he was all right. For the moment I experienced that hallucination or temporal distortion, the fear gripped me that I may be actually stuck in the past, never to see my family again. I was just relieved it was either not real or had been temporary. I had an overwhelming need to see Sarah and our kids, but Steve was the only one within reach. I'd call Sarah as soon as I could, just to hear her voice. As we approached the camp, I eagerly sought Steve. I saw Doc, crouched next to the cooking fire, working over the huge iron skillet. He was slicing up chicken breasts as they fried. Jake was under the fly. Badger and Daniel were cleaning their muskets. Charlie was at his tent, putting away his equipment. But no Steve.

I unhooked my belt, hung it and my canteen over my tent pole, tugged off my sweat-soaked jacket and draped it upside-down over the crest of the tent. From inside the tent I grabbed the bottle of peroxide and the cloth patches for cleaning my musket.

"So," Jake said as he helped Doc prepare the supper by gathering items onto the table under the fly, "did you see any more ghosts? I take it the ghost regiment didn't make another appearance. You stayed in rank until the end."

I poured peroxide down the barrel of the musket. "No, no ghosts."

He caught something in my voice, perhaps the lingering bits of fear, the memories of the dead that just wouldn't let go. I had put the cross in the watch pocket of my trousers, and paused in cleaning my musket to poke a finger into the pocket. I touched the cold metal, but I wasn't relieved. If it had suddenly vanished I could put it all down to hallucination. Now I still didn't know.

Badger had just put his musket away and ducked under the fly to hear Jake's question. "What's up?" He stared at me, knowing there was something more than I was saying.

Jake waited expectantly.

I slipped the cross from my watch pocket and tossed it to Badger, since he was closer. He snatched it out of the air, then held it up between finger and thumb. Sunlight glittered off its surface.

"So?" he asked.

"I found that," I said, "on a dead Confederate soldier."

The others stopped cleaning their muskets, Daniel and Sam moving closer. Doc stood up, straining with the handle of the huge skillet. He brought the steaming mass under the fly to set it on the table.

"I take it," Jake said, "that you don't mean a fellow reenactor playing dead."

"No," I said with a shake of my head.

"Want to talk about it?" Doc asked as he wiped his hands on the cloth that had wrapped the handle of the skillet. I could tell his offer was for a private consultation as well as for a here and now with everyone present. Everyone but Steve.

So I told them, and everyone came under the fly and sat down to hear, rifles forgotten, dinner forgotten.

"I knew it," Jake said, "I just knew something like that could happen when Steve told us about the ghost appearing through those time anomalies. He didn't think it could happen, but I knew it."

"Frank," Sam said, puzzled, "I was right beside you all the time. You didn't go anywhere. When I got up, you were looking at that little cross. I thought you found it on the ground or something."

Badger passed the cross to Jake then wound his thick fingers through his beard. "I don't think quantum theories explain what's going on. I've been thinking about things, and I think something else is going on, something really strange."

"That's obvious," I said.

Jake held up the cross. "Doesn't look that unusual. This was on that dead soldier? Boy, it isn't enough you see ghost regiments and ghost ladies, you have to see the whole battlefield."

"There are no ghosts," Badger said evenly.

"That's what I've been saying," I agreed.

Doc took the cross next. "What do you think, Frank?" he asked.

"What do I think I've been seeing? I haven't been seeing ghosts. Like Badger said, there's no such thing as ghosts. Did I actually travel through time? I don't know. Maybe I became the ghost and made an appearance there like Rebecca Ramsey did to me. More than likely I imagined the whole thing."

Doc lifted up the silver cross. "This is real."

"But can you tell where it came from?" I demanded. "It could be modern. There's no date on it, but that's no guarantee. Sutlers have modern things with nineteenth century dates on them. I could have found it lying on the ground and just imagined the whole battlefield thing. My sense of reality hasn't exactly been reliable this weekend."

"Or maybe it has," Badger said. "Something's going on here, and it ain't good."

Doc passed the cross back to me and looked over at Badger. "You got some idea?"

"Yeah. It may sound weird, but ..." He trailed off.

"Weirder than what?" I asked, considering all the theories flying around. Then I noticed he wasn't looking at any of us. His eyes were on something outside our little camp.

A long shadow pushed its way into our midst.

"This was on that dead soldier?"

I turned to see two men in uniforms out of a different century. It took a few moments to recognize what these men were and what their uniforms meant. When they said nothing but just stood looking around at us, it became apparent that they were not our regular tourists. The stern expressions on their faces were enough to brush that thought away. One was older, a large black man with hair like iron filings. The other was in his twenties, thick biceps almost tearing the short sleeves of his shirt, his hair trimmed so short that he looked bald under his cap.

Jake stood and took a step toward them. "Can we help you?" he asked.

Both men in sheriff uniforms ignored him and zeroed in on Badger.

"Are you called Badger?" the older man asked.

Badger eyed them with suspicion that probably extended from his old life. "Yep."

"I'm Sheriff Ellis and this is Deputy Jackson. We'd like you to come with us, sir," the man said. "We have some questions for you."

Daniel stood up. The rest of us followed suit to surround Badger.

"What's this about?" Daniel asked.

"This doesn't concern you, sir," the sheriff said. He eyed Daniel with exasperation that verged on contempt. I recalled Daniel's earlier encounter with the woman who had insulted him. Sheriff Ellis might have a similar regard for Daniel's participation in our unit.

Daniel's eyes narrowed and his fingers flexed. I hoped he wasn't about to blow up and make matters worse. "I'm making it my concern," he said sharply. "I'm his lawyer."

The sheriff placed his hands on his hips. A small smile pushed on his broad face. "Fine. You can meet us at the sheriff's station." He turned to Badger. "Sir, please come with us."

Daniel stepped closer, coming between him and Badger. He raised his hand. "Hold on, sheriff. You still didn't answer my question. What's this about?"

"Murder, counselor." The sheriff smiled more broadly, but it carried a chill on the humid air. "It's about murder."

Daniel tried to talk several times, then finally managed a croak. "What?"

The sheriff said, "We are investigating a tip, concerning a murder in Georgia ten years ago. Now, we just want to ask some questions. Please come along with us," he said to Badger.

"I ride along," Daniel said.

The sheriff looked at him with open distaste. "That's not how it's done, counselor."

Daniel stood his ground, straightening and becoming taller. "That's how it's going to be, Sheriff. Either that, or I drive Badger over to your office at our discretion. Are you arresting him? Do you have a warrant?"

The sheriff waved his hand. "Have it your way. Come along."

"Let me get my cell phone," Daniel said. He hurried to his tent, coming right back out with his hands full of wallet, cell, and keys. He threw the keys to me and said, "Bring my jeep over, will you, Frank? This shouldn't take long to straighten out."

I caught his keys out of the air. As he trudged out of camp beside the lumbering Badger, flanked by the sheriff and his deputy, I wished I shared his confidence. The sheriff had been serious, and Badger was strangely solemn. He never protested the charge. I recalled what little he had mentioned about his former life riding with that gang. Drugs, violence. What had he done that he couldn't tell me about? Did it include murder?

Chapter Ten

Remember not the sins of my youth, nor my transgressions: according to thy mercy remember thou me for thy goodness' sake, O Lord ... Psalms 25:7

The sheriff's station was on Main Street, a small brick building nestled between the town hall and the bank, both of which were built in the early eighteen hundreds. The station was more modern, with a drive along the bank side to the parking lot in the rear, an extension of the lot behind the town hall. Two dark blue patrol cars sat next to the rear of the sheriff's building, large white letters across the doors spelling out SHERIFF. I parked Daniel's SUV in a slot marked in faded yellow for visitors, then walked back to the front of the building. The main entrance opened into a waiting area with plastic chairs reminiscent of a doctor's waiting room. A heavy metal door led to the inner offices and behind a window sat a receptionist. Again, it reminded me of a doctor's office, except that the window was bulletproof and the young woman at the desk beyond it wore the khaki uniform of a deputy.

"Hi," I said to the woman.

She glanced up from her computer. She looked like she was just out of high school, except for the no-nonsense expression on her tan face. Her blond hair was cropped short and she glared at me with reluctance at having been disturbed. "Yes?" she asked sharply, her voice muffled and coming through a speaker in the bulletproof glass.

"I'm here for Badg—" It occurred to me that I didn't know Badger's real name, or at least his surname. I'd sound like an idiot asking for a woodland creature. "I'm here for Daniel Meyers, the attorney."

"He's with his client. Have a seat." She returned her attention to her flat-screen and keyboard, giving me no more concern.

I sat in a hard, uncomfortable plastic chair and had to shift my position every few minutes to prevent myself from sliding off the chair's slick surface.

A buzzer sounded, metal tumblers clicked, and the heavy door beside the window slid open. Daniel pushed through and Deputy Jackson pulled the door shut behind him.

I jumped to my feet. "What's going on? Where's Badger?"

Daniel shook his head and rifled through a yellow legal pad he carried. A dozen pages were scrawled upon, and I wondered where he had gotten it. The sheriff must have supplied it for him. He hadn't brought one from camp.

"It's not good, Frank. I'm in over my head with this."

"With what? What's going on?" I must have raised my voice because out of the corner of my eye I saw the deputy behind the window lift her head to eye us.

Daniel glanced at the yellow pages. "Well, the deceased is William Kowalski, a.k.a. Billy Laski, a.k.a. the Bull. He was a member of the Warriors, the gang Badger rode with. Ten years ago, in Kimble, Georgia, he was killed from multiple stab wounds. That also happens to be the last time members of the Warriors saw Badger, until yesterday."

"They're accusing Badger?" I asked.

He shook his head. "Not at the moment. They're being very careful about that, but then this isn't their investigation. They're just holding him to see if they need to extradite him to Georgia. They're just questioning him."

I lifted my hands. "Well then, where is he? Are they holding him?"

He folded his papers back over the pad. "They can hold him overnight without charging him."

"Can't you get him out?"

"Look, Frank, I'm not a criminal lawyer. I'm doing the best I can. This isn't exactly my expertise, and I don't want to screw it up. Badger's my friend, too. But he isn't helping much right now."

"What do you mean? You don't think he actually did it?" Considering we only knew Badger for the past couple of years, I was afraid that he might be guilty. He could be one frightening guy. I didn't want to believe that, though. Even with his background with the Warriors, he was still a good person. I couldn't see Badger, in all his terrible girth, stabbing a man over and over.

Daniel lifted his hands and looked at me with an apologetic look. "I just don't know. That was a rough time in his life. He even admits he's done some bad things. He was a different person then."

"Yeah, but murder? That I can't believe."

"Well, he says he knew this Kowalski, but hadn't seen him since he left the gang. Unfortunately, that's the same day, or close to it, that Kowalski died. Not a very good alibi."

I flexed my fingers and tapped my foot. I shoved my hands into my pockets, felt a set of keys in the right side, and pulled them out. I swung them unconsciously around my finger. When I realized they were Daniel's keys, I tossed them to him. There had to be something I could do. I just couldn't sit back and let this happen to Badger. I knew he was innocent. There was more to this than what we knew. I had to learn more, I had to find out why he was singled out. "I want to talk to him," I told Daniel.

"You aren't his lawyer. You can't."

I snatched the legal pad out of his hand. "I'm your assistant. Get back in there to talk to him."

Daniel stared down at his empty fingers, then he heaved a heavy sigh, lowered his head, and pinched the bridge of his nose. "Frank, it's late. Let's go back to camp and let Badger think things over. Maybe a night in a cell will clear his mind and make him a bit more cooperative."

I folded my arms over my chest, the yellow pad dangling from one hand, and stared Daniel down.

He held up his hands in surrender. "All right."

Ten minutes later, we were in the bare interrogation room that smelled of stale coffee and cigarettes, seated around the steel table with Badger. Deputy Jackson stood outside the room, occasionally glancing in through the reinforced glass window in the steel door.

"Badger," Daniel began, opening his pad to a blank page, "I just want to ask some questions about the situation, just to get your point of view."

"Did you kill the guy?" I asked, my hands flat on the table between us, my eyes glaring into Badger's face, trying to hold his gaze.

Daniel groaned. "Frank! Let me do this."

Badger looked at me steadily now, then pursed his lips beneath the shaggy beard. "No," he said finally.

"Then what's this all about?" I demanded. "Level with Daniel. He's trying to help. The least you can do is help him help you."

He shrugged his big shoulders. "Who'd believe me? The sheriff is already convinced I'm guilty. Wouldn't surprise me none if he had papers already filled out to send me down to Georgia. He made up his mind as soon as he saw me. Even Daniel has his doubts."

"Well, what did you expect," Daniel said. "You won't even talk to me, and I'm your lawyer."

Badger grinned, his uneven teeth poking through the whiskers. "And how many murder trials have you done?"

A scowl flashed over Daniel's face, then he shook his head in exasperation.

Then Badger wagged a finger at me. "But you didn't think I done it, did you, Frank?"

"No," I said, my anger starting to wane. "Not that I couldn't be wrong. But I know you, Badger. You couldn't."

His smile vanished in a flash and his face became hard. "You didn't know me then. I wasn't the same person. I've done some pretty rotten things. I told you so."

"And you just said you didn't kill this Kowalski guy," I said.

He shrugged again. "Don't make no difference. Can't get away from what I used to be. To people like that sheriff I'm still a biker. You think the police in Georgia are goin' to think any different?"

"Is that the way your pastor sees you?" I asked.

He looked down at his huge scarred hands. "No."

"Neither do I," I said.

"Ditto," Daniel said.

"And that goes for Steve, and the rest of the guys."

He nodded slowly.

I rubbed my hands together. "Okay. Now let's get you out of this mess. So you knew Kowalski and probably left the Warriors about the same time he met his end. Did you know he was killed?"

Badger shook his head. "Nope. I left them and went north, never heard anything about any of 'em until yesterday. I went on my own. Never wanted to see 'em again. Got sick of that life. Rode off on my own, got some odd jobs, eventually made it to PA, and eventually scraped enough money together for my own business."

Daniel poised his pencil over his pad, then decided against putting anything down. He wagged the pencil back and forth like a little fan.

"Okay," I said. "That doesn't help. How about going back a little. What was your relationship with Kowalski?"

"We rode together."

"And ...?" I prompted.

He lifted his hands. "It was like a family. Dysfunctional, yeah. You got along with some and not with others. There were fights and we fought other gangs."

"Yeah, but what about Kowalski? You didn't get along with him, did you? Did you ever fight?"

"Sure. That's what bein' a biker's like. I fought with just about everyone in the gang. Even Jewel and me had a few knock-downs. Ain't unusual."

"Yes," Daniel said, "but someone decided to poke him several times with a knife. That's a little different from a family squabble."

Badger rolled his eyes and smirked.

"You think he deserved it, don't you?" I said.

He shook his head and his eyes grew sad. "He weren't no angel, but he didn't deserve what he got. Now he's burning in hell for the rest of eternity. I wouldn't want that even for the Bull. He was a son of a —." He stopped suddenly and looked at each of us, surprise on his face. "You see? Can't get away from what I was. I hadn't sworn in years. Took years to break that habit, and one day to get right back in."

"Not quite," I said. "You stopped yourself. You're a new creature, remember?"

He sighed, not quite willing to grant the truth of my words.

"Okay," I said, steering us back on track. "He wasn't a likable guy and you didn't like him. So, why would anyone think you made a pin cushion out of him?"

"We ... argued the day I left. We was staying at an abandoned farm, living in the run-down farm house and the barn. There was about twenty of us, give or take. Someone had just brought in a load of weed and we was all tokin'. It just wasn't doing anything for me. And I was tired of the booze. It'd been bothering me for some time, but I stuck around. Didn't have nowhere else to go. But I figured there had to be something else. I just got fed up and left."

"Whoa," I said, holding up my hands to form a T. "You skipped a few things. Like, about the argument with this guy. Care to tell us about it? It might pertain to his murder, or at least you being accused of it."

"Weren't important."

"I beg to differ." I was close to losing my temper. This was harder than getting a straight answer from a teenager, and I've dealt with hundreds of them.

"Okay," he said finally, letting out air so that he actually looked like he deflated. "It was over a girl. He put moves on my girl. We had it out. He backed down. Case closed."

"Not so easily," I said. "Care for a little more detail? Are we talking about your former friend Jewel?"

"Yeah. The Bull got her stoned, then put moves on her. I caught them in one of the rooms in the old house and laid into him. Turned out ... turned out it weren't all his fault. She led him on."

"Ah!" I sat back and passed a hand through my hair. Someone in the room needed a shower and I thought it was me. I didn't say anything for a time. Now I understood why he left the gang. It wasn't solely because he got fed up with the lifestyle.

"Yeah," he said eventually. "I thought Jewel and me were, y'know. That just flipped me out. I weren't going to stay there and be made a fool, so I packed my stuff and rode off."

"Anyone see you leave?" Daniel asked, pencil poised.

"Yep. Jewel was there, standing on the porch, watching me go. Never said a word. The Bull was still in the house, with about a dozen other people, most of 'em stoned or asleep."

"This fight you had, did either of you have a knife?" I asked.

"Nah. We just pounded each other. I might have broke his nose. He gave me a shiner. That's about it. I just wanted to get outta there. They just made me into one big jerk. He was fine when I rode off."

"Then why would the Georgia police think you killed him?" I asked.

Daniel shuffled his papers. "Ah, according to their reports at the time, Badger took off after he was killed. Not the most reliable witnesses, fellow members of the Warriors. As far as the sheriff volunteered, there really isn't any evidence against Badger. He's been wanted for questioning for ten years."

"And who said he left after Kowalski was killed?" I asked Daniel.

He shrugged. "I didn't get that. I don't have a copy of the report."

I rubbed my eyes and suddenly something that had been gnawing at the back of my brain leaped out at me. "And who let the sheriff know he was here? I mean, I doubt the sheriff was looking for Badger just because of a ten-year-old police report from another state. It's not like his picture's been on the Ten Most Wanted all these years. Someone had to have put the sheriff onto him."

Daniel shrugged again. I glared at him and he huffed through his nose. "Give me a break, Frank. I'm not a criminal lawyer. I haven't done anything like this since law school. Personally, I think we should get Badger a better lawyer. I know a few back home, and I can make some calls. I was planning on doing that after we met with the sheriff. Badger will be out first thing in the morning."

"Not good enough," I said.

"Hey Frank," Badger said. "It ain't no big deal. I've been in the tank longer than that."

"No," I said vehemently. "You're getting out tonight."

I swung the door open so hard that the deputy on guard, leaning against it, nearly fell in. He straightened and glared at me, his hand dropping to cover the butt of his automatic.

"Get the sheriff," I said.

"He's having his dinner."

"Get him anyway."

He scowled at me, then called down the hall. "Hey Cindy, can you buzz the sheriff? These guys want to see him."

I couldn't hear if the deputy at the front desk made a reply. Jackson pulled the door shut and left us for about ten minutes. When the door opened again, it framed Sheriff Ellis, who was not in the best of moods at having his dinner interrupted.

"What do you want now?" he demanded.

"Answers," I said, echoing his tone. I probably ran the risk of being thrown in a cell adjoining Badger's, but I didn't much care at the moment.

He eased out a heavy sigh, folded his arms over his chest, and glared.

"Look," I said in a more reasonable tone, "someone informed you that our friend was wanted for questioning in Georgia. Who was it?"

He looked over at Daniel. "I thought you were his lawyer. Who's this? Your co-counsel?"

"In a way," I said. Could he arrest me for practicing law without a license? All I was trying to do was get some answers. "Who told you about the murder in Georgia?"

"I don't have to tell you that," he said.

"Actually," Daniel said, straightening his glasses, "you do."

The sheriff rolled his eyes. "I don't have time for this. You can wait 'til the morning." He started to turn.

"You had enough time to come into our camp and arrest Badger," I pointed out. "You didn't even bother to send just a deputy, but you came yourself. You spared an hour to question him. All of a sudden, you don't have time?"

He spun on me and jabbed his finger like he was hurling a javelin toward my heart. "I don't have time for people like you, who wave your Confederate flag around like a banner. You can wait 'til morning."

I started laughing.

Daniel stared at me. He looked like he wanted to crawl under the table and hide. The sheriff glared at me, his jaw twisting as he ground his teeth in anger. Badger smiled just slightly.

"Son," the sheriff said tightly, "maybe you want to spend the night in our facilities."

I wagged my finger at the sheriff. "You think that because we're Confederate reenactors, we're white supremacists or something like that. Is that it? Just because we use the Confederate flag, you lump us all together with bigots. Am I right?"

"You glorify slavery," he said. His words nearly hissed through his teeth.

Daniel leaped up, his eyes flashing. "No we don't! How dare you think that! That is the most prejudicial thing I've ever heard. Reenacting isn't a place for racists. We're historians. We glorify history. If you think otherwise, you are the narrow-minded bigot! Slavery was a terrible institution, and nothing can change that, but that wasn't the only driving force of the war or the trouble between the North and the South."

"Daniel," I said softly.

"Do a little reading, Sheriff, and maybe you'll learn something. Do you think I've turned my back on my people? I'm as black as you and my ancestors came over here the same way yours did. They were slaves, too, but one of my ancestors was a freed man who fought on the side of the South to protect his land. He—"

"Daniel!"

He stopped mid-word with his mouth open, blinking like he had just awakened from a strange dream. He closed his mouth and sat back down. "Sorry."

"So," the sheriff said, raising his chin and pursing his lips, "you had an ancestor who fought for the South?"

"Yes," Daniel said in a calmer tone, as though he had just shaken himself free of a convulsion, "Jeremiah Livingston, born in Winchester, Virginia. He rose to the rank of corporal and survived the war. His little farm, which he had fought for, was burned to the ground the last months of the war. Carpetbaggers gave the property to freed slaves during the Restoration period."

"Don't know about my own people back then," the sheriff said. "They were slaves, I know that much, and some bitter memories come up through the generations. But we don't have any records. Okay, Counselor, you made your point. Maybe I jumped to conclusions, but I've had to deal with a lot of bigotry all my life. Maybe you're too young and maybe you never ran into trouble up North, but I have here and further south. Bigots, racists, supremacists, the Klan. I've had it all, since I was little. We've had cross burnings, church burnings, beatings, and worse. Maybe where you live it's just history, but in the South we still live it and most of us don't like it."

"There's a lot of twisted people out there, Sheriff," Daniel said, "and they are not restricted to the South. But that's not why my friends and I reenact the Civil War. There's more to the war than the issue of slavery."

The sheriff threw out his hands. "Hold on, Counselor. Let's not go there again. I'll take your view into consideration as long as you can see my point, too."

"Sure." Daniel nodded.

"How about Badger," I said, motioning to the man still sitting silently at the table. "Someone let you know about the murder in Georgia and that Badger was here."

He nodded. "Yes. Someone called in from a payphone and gave us the information, but she didn't leave her name."

"She?" I said. "A woman?"

"Yes, but like I said, she didn't leave her name. She let us know about the ten-year-old murder and that your friend was wanted for questioning. I wasn't going to bother, but she sounded pretty insistent, said he might be dangerous, so I checked it out. I had the report emailed to me before I considered doing anything."

I glanced over at Badger. "Well, we can guess who made the call."

He wouldn't look at me.

"Doesn't matter," the sheriff said. "The report from Georgia gives his description and his alias, if not his actual name. He was described by witnesses as having fought with the victim, then fled the state after his death."

"But he left before that."

"Not according to witnesses."

"And who were the witnesses?" I asked.

Sheriff Ellis looked at Daniel. "Now just who is the lawyer here?" But before Daniel could say anything, the sheriff left.

In a few moments he returned with a printout that carried the Georgia state seal in its corner. "Two witnesses named," he said, reading from the printout. "Elizabeth Jenkins and Morris Stein."

I looked over at Badger, but he just shrugged. "Who the heck are they?" I asked.

"Witnesses," the sheriff said, as though I missed the obvious. "They made statements when the state police investigated the murder."

"Maybe I can guess who one of them is," I said. "What if you had a talk with her?"

"Mister," the sheriff began, "this isn't my problem. This is Georgia's case, not mine. Take it up with them."

"No. You took my friend. This is your problem, and we're going to help you deal with it." I marched out of the room.

I made it to Daniel's SUV before I realized I had given him back his keys.

*****

Daniel pulled his SUV into the gravel parking lot of the bar. It looked much the same as it had the night before, with possibly more trucks. It was not as late as my last visit and the sun still squinted over the mountains, giving an ominous red cast. I stepped out of the jeep and stared at the metal front door. Daniel pulled away to find a parking space, and I felt abandoned once more. I felt that the next time I would see him would be when he paid me a visit in the hospital. But Badger was in trouble and this was the only way I knew to get him out of it.

They weren't at the same table they had used the night before. I looked around in the gloom, waiting for my eyes to adjust, my ears stinging from the pounding of the loud music, and found many eyes staring back at me. There were more customers than before, and most looked even more dangerous than those from yesterday. It looked like all the inmates had just escaped from a local penitentiary. This was probably the dumbest thing I had ever done.

I should have gotten out while I could still walk.

Diablo's guffaw boomed over the sounds of the jukebox, emanating from a deep dark corner.

This definitely wasn't a good idea.

"Hey look! It's the professor."

The voice sounded like Diablo's skinny companion, coming from the same corner.

"Come here, professor, *mi amigo*." Diablo's tone was not as friendly as his words, but at least they were slurred with alcohol.

He was at a large table with the thin man and other bikers dressed in leather and tattoos. Three were women in tight leather vests and jeans or cut-offs and fewer tattoos. One sitting close to Diablo had a tattoo vine encircling her muscular biceps, a thorn appearing to pierce her brown skin and draw inked blood. At the far end of the table sat Red and Jewel.

"What do you want?" Diablo demanded.

"Who's this, babe?" asked the woman next to him. She wrapped one hand over his thickly muscled arm and the other hand around a beer bottle.

"Nobody. Just some teacher thinks he's tough enough to cross us. You ain't no Seal, are you, professor?"

My attention stayed on Jewel. "Nope."

One biker with a belly that pushed up his tee shirt slammed his beer bottle onto the table. "You want I should take him out back, Diablo?"

Diablo shook his head. "No. We have a little fun later. What do you want, professor? I ain't askin' again."

"I'm here to help Badger," I said and walked toward the other end of the table.

"Your *amigo* Badger ain't here, so no one here to help you. We have some fun tonight."

"Hey, look," said the skinny guy, "another one."

I turned and looked over my shoulder. Daniel came across the barroom, an apprehensive look on his face. I could guess why. He was the only black man in the place. I had thought I would feel better with him backing me up, but the situation seemed to get worse. Some men were openly scowling at him. I wondered how many were white supremacists or just plain racists.

"Came as quickly as I could," Daniel said as he caught up with me, a weak smile flashing over his face. He pushed his glasses up his nose. "Had to make a quick phone call."

I turned my attention back toward Jewel and said, "I want to talk to you, Elizabeth."

Her face paled and she lost the malevolent grin she had been wearing. Beside her, Red's bleary eyes took on a quizzical expression. He glanced from her to me, while she stared with a slack jaw.

"How did ..." Her words trailed off.

"Elizabeth Jenkins," I said. "I want to talk to you about Badger."

She shook herself. "I can't help you."

"You're the one who called the sheriff and told him he was here," I said, my voice rising in anger above the booming country-western music. "You were the one who told the police in Georgia that he left the state after Kowalski was killed."

"Who?" she asked.

"Kowalski. The Bull. You made him the prime suspect in a murder ten years ago. Now he's waiting to be sent to Georgia to be arrested. I thought Badger was your friend, but you lied to get him in trouble, maybe send him to prison. Some friend you are."

She stuttered, then her face flushed. "He left me. He ran out on me."

"After he caught you and the Bull together. You betrayed his trust. Worse, you made a fool of him. What choice did you give him?"

"He killed the Bull," she said, her voice shaky, becoming angry.

"You know he didn't. You know when he left. You watched him go. But you lied to the police. Maybe you even know who really did it."

"You don't understand. Me and Badger, we were tight. But he didn't own me. I took what came to me. Ain't no crime in that. Badger would've done the same after a while. I was ready, he wasn't."

"But you lied. Did you do that to get even with him?" I asked. I saw her eyes flash and knew I had struck a nerve. "You were angry with him for leaving, so you decided to get even. Except he could end up in prison. And I bet you were mad he left you last night, too. That's why you called the local sheriff's office to tip them off that a man wanted in connection with a murder was sitting in the battlefield. You rejected Badger but you couldn't stand it when he rejected you."

"Hey, man!" Red said. "Get lost. Leave her alone."

A chorus of profanity rang out along the table, picked up by the tables nearby.

Diablo stood slowly. "I think it's time we teach the teacher a lesson. *Si?*" He smacked one huge fist into the palm of his other hand. It sounded like a tree snapping in half.

"Just relax," I said, a little sharper than I wanted to, which probably wasn't the best thing to do in this particular situation.

He grinned, his gold tooth catching the light. "Or what. I get detention, professor? I don't think your colored friend's going to help you none."

"Yeah." Red stood, his hand coming out from under his leather vest. I saw the shaft of a folded knife, a switchblade. He moved fast for his size, probably from a lifetime of fights.

"What about us?" someone asked.

I recognized the voice. I turned reluctantly from Red and saw Jake with his arms folded over his chest. And Doc, Sam, and Charlie. Behind them came the clank of more brogans as other reenactors entered the bar. There were the guys from Company H, and more behind them. Even Colonel Wessner was among them.

"Is there a problem here?" Doc asked.

"Hey!" yelled the bartender. "I don't want no trouble. You guys get out or I call the cops."

I doubted that half the customers would want the police called in. Diablo sat back down but glared at me. Then I heard the metallic snap.

I caught Red's movement out of the corner of my eye, his thick arm swinging at me. I turned to get out of his way and heard the swish of his hand cutting through the air. I collided with an empty chair. I grabbed it and swung it around to put it between the crazed creature and myself. Red stumbled towards me, his eyes red from intoxication. He was not on a scale approaching Diablo or Badger, and he was not in good shape, but he was larger than I. And he was armed. But he was drunk and probably under the influence of various illegal chemicals. He overcompensated with a lunge, lost his balance, tangled himself in the chair, and crashed heavily downward. The back of the chair cracked and the legs splintered. The switchblade clattered across the floor. Red tumbled down with a grunt, sending the fractured chair skidding.

"Frank!" I heard someone yell. It sounded like Jake.

Daniel snatched up the knife before Red could grab it again. Jake and Sam grabbed hold of Red, putting their combined weight on him to pin him, face down. He kicked his feet but couldn't get up. He let loose with a series of profanity that went mostly into the dirty boards of the floor.

"Hold on, Frank," Doc shouted, and I wondered what he was so excited about. Doc hardly ever gets flustered unless something starts burning in his skillet. He was at my side before I realized it, lifting my arm to examine my side. "It's not deep. Should be okay." He pushed something against my side and a surge of pain shot through me.

"Owww!" I cried. "What are you doing?" I looked down to see my shirt torn and soaked with blood. My side stung, but it hadn't hurt until Doc pressed some cloth against it. Red had sliced me but he hadn't been able to stab me. I came very close to having some major damage.

Daniel wagged the knife at the bartender. "I believe now would be an appropriate time to call the police."

Some patrons were discretely slipping out the door.

I held Doc's makeshift bandage against my wound and turned to Jewel again. She was up and moving away in a hurry, but I caught her arm. My fingers were slick with my own blood and her wrist slid under my grasp. I felt the steel cords of her muscles. She could have easily broken my hand, let alone my grip, but she stopped. "You have a second chance, Elizabeth. You have the opportunity to help Badger by telling the truth. Make another statement. Tell the sheriff Badger couldn't have killed Kowalski."

"What's it to you, man?" she demanded, her eyes burning into mine like twin torches of rage and pain. "He's not one of you. He doesn't belong with the likes of you."

"You're wrong. He's my friend. We're all his friends," I said, nodding my head toward the other reenactors. "What about you?"

She squeezed her eyes tight, then looked back at me with a sadness that flashed for a moment and was gone. "He used to be," she said.

Chapter Eleven

Buy the truth, and sell it not; also wisdom, and instruction, and understanding … Proverbs 23:23

The plastic chair in the waiting area of the sheriff's office was uncomfortable and I kept sliding down in it. I was afraid that if I dozed off I would soon end up on the floor. Beside me, Doc seemed to have made peace with his chair and they had developed a symbiotic relationship. He kept the chair warm and the chair kept him in place. My seat was not so reasonable. I continually shifted to remain upright.

"You need to go to the emergency room," Doc said. I lost track of how many times he had said that. And of the times he checked my wound under his field dressings.

"I'm fine." I was just tired. "Besides, do you doubt your own talents?"

"Of course not. But you need a tetanus shot. No telling where that knife's been. That guy probably uses it to clean his fingernails."

"I doubt that. Did you see his fingernails? I doubt they've ever been clean. Red doesn't impress me as one for personal hygiene."

"My point exactly," Doc insisted. "Who knows what could be on that knife of his if he takes such good care of himself. You need to get to the hospital right away. You need stitches."

I felt his field dressing under my torn shirt. My side was sore, but it

"You need to go to the emergency room."

didn't feel that bad. I felt worse over my shirt. Torn and stained with my own blood, it would make for a good show on the next battlefield. Too bad it was my favorite shirt. "I'll go," I conceded. "After we hear from Daniel and after I see Steve." I expected Steve was back at camp by now, but I wanted to make certain. I didn't like him riding around town at night with the likes of Diablo on the loose. Neither of us had a cell phone to call anyone back at camp in order for me to check on him.

Jake had wanted to stay with us, but I had insisted he return to camp to wait for Steve. I didn't want Steve returning to find the camp deserted. And night had fallen. Someone needed to light the lanterns so we could find our way back.

Daniel finally came out with the sheriff. The sheriff was shaking his head, but Daniel was smiling.

I stood up. "What about Badger?"

The sheriff waved an impatient hand. "Hold on, son. Your lady friend made her statement and the state police down in Georgia got a faxed copy. They're going over it, but they may not make any decision until Monday. This is Saturday night, remember. And they still might want us to ship your friend down for questioning. But there is something interesting that we found out about the one who tried to stab you."

Daniel bounced on the heels of his brogans. "His real name is Morris Stein."

I frowned. "That sounds familiar."

"It's the other witness against your friend," the sheriff said. "He and Ms. Jenkins both made statements against your friend. But it seems Mr. Stein is wanted in Kentucky for a stabbing. No fatality, but injuries from a bar fight. Seems to me that he might have had something to do with Kowalski's murder. The autopsy report said the weapon used was consistent with a large switchblade."

My skin crawled. I might have been cut with a murder weapon.

"Mr. Stein," the sheriff continued, "will be spending some time here, then we'll see if Georgia wants him. He's very cooperative. We might even get a confession out of him. That would put a nice ending on my day. What's left of it. The Jenkins woman, by the way, said you were one crazy … well, I won't repeat the phrase, but you'll get the picture."

"Yeah," I said. Crazy was right. I see things, talk to dead people, throw myself at homicidal bikers. "I'm just glad she decided to talk to you."

"I think she was starting to worry about that Stein fellow," Sheriff Ellis said. "She pretty much knew he killed that man in Georgia, and she knew about his bar fights. He could get pretty mean, I guess. When she was starting to hang around your friend again, he was getting jealous. I think she was worried he'd stab her next time. He could have stabbed you."

"I got lucky."

"Well, get out of here. I don't want you bleeding on my floor." He suddenly looked up at the main entrance. "What the ..."

A number of people pushed through into the waiting area. A tall, distinguished man led two deputies and two teenagers. The young blond-haired girl was keeping up a running dialogue, with the tall man trying to interrupt in an angry voice. After a moment I recognized Merryweather, once again in his Confederate general's uniform, his face burning red behind his trim gray beard. Jenna was disheveled. Steve remained quiet, his mouth drawn into a thin straight line.

"Steve!" I shouted. This was the last place I expected to see him, unless Jake was bringing him over. Well, Harley's was actually the last place I expected to see him, but the sheriff's office was a close second.

Jenna fell suddenly quiet in mid-sentence and Steve looked up at me in surprise; then he flushed with embarrassment.

"Hi, Dad." His soft tone reminded me of the time he broke a window while target practicing with a homemade slingshot.

At least he wasn't handcuffed, but the attitude of the deputies was that he should be.

"What's going on?" I demanded.

"Ah, Frank Blaine," Merryweather said. "Good of you to meet us here. I just caught your son in the act of breaking and entering. He and my granddaughter were in my den, going through my personal papers. I immediately called the police. I intend to press charges if my papers are not returned."

"That's not true," Jenna said. "We didn't break in. We used a key. And we didn't take any of your papers. We were just doing some research."

Merryweather wagged his finger at her. "You were in my house without my permission, young lady. You were in my den and going through papers I have for my own research."

"Okay, okay," the sheriff shouted, waving his hands for attention. "One thing at a time. Mr. Merryweather, I suppose you called us. What's the complaint?"

Merryweather scowled in impatience. "I just explained that, Sheriff. I came home and found these two in my den. At least one item is missing. I want to file a complaint. I want this boy arrested unless that item is returned."

"What item?" the sheriff asked.

"A journal. Very old," Merryweather explained. "Very important to my historical research."

"Do you have this journal, son?" the sheriff asked Steve.

"No, sir," he said. I had no doubt that he told the truth but I could also tell he was hiding something, not volunteering the whole truth. Over the years I have learned to ask the right questions in order to reach the whole truth. Sometime it was a long, involved process of leading questions. Sheriff Ellis might not have the advantage of my years of experience in interrogations. It proved handy in high school.

"How about you, miss?" asked the sheriff.

Jenna started to speak, shaking her head, then stopped. "Ah, well." She hesitated, then reached under her tee shirt and pulled out the small book.

"Do you realize how old that is, young lady?" Merryweather snapped. "That book should be in a museum. It is a piece of antiquity, and you shove it in your jeans like it's a comic book."

I was about to tell him that some comic books are probably worth more than that journal but I felt it wasn't the time to bring up that little bit of trivia.

He tried to snatch the journal from her hand, but Jenna pulled away. "No! This isn't yours. It belongs to Mrs. Letterman."

The sheriff stepped in and gently took the journal from Jenna's fingers. "Mrs. Letterman, eh? Is that right, Mr. Merryweather?"

"Well, yes. It belongs to her. She has allowed me to borrow it in order to do my research. It has been entrusted into my care, and this boy has stolen it."

"It would seem," the sheriff said as he opened the book to glance over some pages, "that your granddaughter stole it. It was in her possession."

"But Steve Blaine was there," Merryweather insisted. "He is guilty of breaking and entering."

Daniel tapped the sheriff on the shoulder. "Ah, excuse me, sheriff, but if charges are to be made against my client, Mr. Blaine, then they must also be made against Miss Connor, since they were both caught inside Mr. Merryweather's house without permission."

The sheriff nodded his head sagely. He closed the book and continued to hold it in front of him with both hands. "Yes sir, counselor. They must both be guilty. I'll have to arrest both of them. Mr. Merryweather?"

I imagined the headlines in the local paper, concerning a banker having his own granddaughter arrested for entering his house. That might be enough to turn customers toward a rival financial institution.

"Both?" Merryweather said, his face paling. Maybe he imagined the same headlines. "You can't arrest my granddaughter. In fact, as long as I have the journal back, I won't press charges." He held his hand out toward the sheriff.

The sheriff ignored him and looked down at the worn leather cover. "You admit that this belongs to Mrs. Letterman?"

"Of course. I said she has allowed me to use it in my research."

"And he's kept it," Jenna said. "She wants it back and asked if we'd return it to her. We talked to her this afternoon."

"That's ridiculous," Merryweather said, extending his hand again.

The sheriff walked back to the bulletproof window and the same deputy that had been on duty earlier. "Cindy, give Margaret Letterman a call. I want to talk with her."

The deputy nodded and began typing on her keyboard. In a moment she was speaking quietly into her headset. The sheriff went through the metal security door and appeared behind his deputy a moment later. She handed him a telephone handset, and we could hear his heavy bass voice coming through the little speaker in the window. It sounded tinny and cartoonish.

"Mrs. Letterman, sorry to bother you this late. Thank you. It's about this old journal Mr. Merryweather borrowed from you. Yes. Two teens. Yes, they are nice children. Thank you, Mrs. Letterman. I'll be sure to tell them."

When he returned, he said, "It seems that Mrs. Letterman has asked a number of times for the journal to be returned. You didn't oblige her, Mr. Merryweather. She's not feeling kindly towards you. She asked your granddaughter and young Mr. Blaine here to return it to her if they came across it. She said Monday would be fine, or tomorrow after church. Now, as far as breaking and entering, if you want to file charges against both of them, we have no choice but to follow through and arrest both of them. It's your call, Mr. Merryweather."

Merryweather fumed. "I'll drop the charges. Go ahead, let them go. But don't expect very much support on your reelection next year, Sheriff."

The sheriff chuckled as Merryweather stormed out of the building, shoving the door out of his way. It hissed gently as it closed behind him. "Well, I wouldn't want his support anyway. Never liked the man." He handed the journal to Jenna. "Take good care of this, young lady. And Mrs. Letterman had better get it in perfect condition as soon as possible."

"Yes sir," she said. "Thank you, Sheriff Ellis."

"Ah, does that mean we can go?" Steve asked.

"Yes," the sheriff said. "Get out of here. I don't want to see any of you again."

The deputy tapped on the glass window to get the sheriff's attention. She held up the phone again. He sighed, disappeared through the door again, and reappeared behind the woman. This time we didn't bother to listen in on his conversation. We headed toward the door in the wake of Merryweather's hurried departure, but a tap on the window brought us all up short. Sheriff Ellis had one finger in the air for us to wait. I wondered what new tragedy would be unfolding. Who else was going to be charged with some crime?

When Sheriff Ellis hung up, he came back through the security door to the waiting room. He chewed on his lower lip before he spoke. "Well, counselor, it seems the Georgia state police aren't interested in talking to your client, your other client, that is. At least for right now. Since he has his own business in Pennsylvania and has been a long-time resident, they feel they can get hold of him if they ever need to. They are, however, interested in Morris Stein. He might be popular in a couple of other states besides Kentucky. We'll release your client in just a little bit, if you want to wait."

*****

Steve and Jenna huddled together on the plastic chairs in the waiting room while we waited for Badger to be released. Jenna cradled the old journal in her hands and Steve gingerly turned the aged, yellow pages as they both read the handwritings of Howard Long. They would stop and talk over a passage or talk over what a particular faded word might be. Certain parts made them more excited.

"Where's my truck?" I asked.

Steve pointed a thumb toward the front entrance. "Out back. Jenna drove it over. The deputies, ah, insisted I ride with them."

I nodded in understanding. "You do have that dangerous criminal kind of look."

"Runs in the family," he said.

"Don't let your mother hear you say that," I warned him.

"Oh yeah," Jenna said. She balanced the journal on one hand and dug into the pocket of her jeans with the other. With some struggle she freed my keys. "Here. I hope you don't mind."

I took the keys from her. "As long as you filled the tank, not at all."

She stared at me.

Steve leaned closer to her. "He's joking. You can tell. He's not smiling."

"Oh." She smiled weakly, then nervously tried to return her attention back to the journal.

"You should read this, Dad," Steve said, jabbing his finger toward the book. "It tells what really happened. I don't know where Mr. Merryweather got his information, but according to Captain Long, that train raid happened totally different."

"That's good," I said, only half-aware of what he was saying.

"What's taking so long?" Daniel asked. He paused in his pacing to glare at the heavy security door. "He should have been out an hour ago."

"I don't know, Daniel," I said. "You're the lawyer. You know all that stuff."

"I keep telling you, I'm not a criminal lawyer. This is the first I've seen of the inside of a police station since law school, and that was because ... ah, well, never mind. All this goes faster in classroom theory. What's taking so long?"

The locks clicked loudly and the door swung open. One of the deputies who had brought Steve in escorted Badger out.

At the same moment, the front door opened and Miranda Connor swirled in with her long dress swishing. She looked much the same as she had the night before at the Ramsey mansion, though now she clutched a heavy knit shawl over her shoulders. Her face was flushed and a few strands of hair had come loose and swayed with her rush to enter.

Her eyes shot to each of us before finding her daughter, who was still engrossed in the journal.

"There you are!" she said.

Jenna looked up. "Oh, hi Mom. I guess you got my message."

"Yes, I did. What a shock to come home to an empty house and find out your daughter is in jail. My word, I should ground you for a month."

Jenna rolled her eyes. "Ah Mom. I'm not in jail. I told you ... well, I left the message that we were at the sheriff's because of a little misunderstanding."

Miranda began pacing, her dress swishing loudly. "Yes, your grandfather stopped by when I was finishing the last ghost tour. He was fit to be tied. He's so angry at you and your friend, he'll probably disinherit you."

"I thought he did that when I moved in with Dad." She drew her chin down and spoke in a deep, pseudo-masculine voice. "'How dare she become a northerner? She's no granddaughter of mine!'"

Steve stifled a laugh.

Miranda's hands flew through the air, unsettling her shawl. "He did not say that, but he might as well have. I swear, what is your father teaching you? I should have a few choice words with him."

Jenna rolled her eyes again.

Miranda pointed to the journal on her daughter's lap. "Is that what all this trouble is about? Your grandfather was carrying on so about this book. Honestly, you had no right to enter his house and take it without permission."

"But we did have permission, from the journal's owner, Mrs. Letterman. She wants it back and Granddad wouldn't return it, so she asked us to see if we could get it back to her."

"That's fine, but going through his things, and when no one was home, no wonder he had such a fit. You're just lucky he didn't press charges. You could be spending the night in jail."

"I'm just glad I'm not spending the night in jail," Badger said, coming through the inner door. He paused to look at everyone. "I miss something? What's been happening? What happened to your shirt, Frank?"

"Just going for realism," I said, tugging on the torn material. The stain had dried to a reddish-brown.

Badger huffed. "Wrong color for blood. You need some of that stage blood they sell at the sutlers."

Doc laughed. "I told him it wasn't real enough."

"Isn't that your best shirt?" Steve asked. He bent his head and studied the slash and the bandage underneath. His eyes widened.

"Dad! What happened?"

"It's a long story," I said. "I'm all right."

"He needs to have it looked at," Doc said. "But he wouldn't leave until he saw you and until Badger got released."

Badger slammed a beefy hand on my shoulder. "Thanks for waiting. Thought you guys would be in bed by now. Thanks, Daniel, for the legal-eagle stuff. Send me a bill."

Daniel waved him off. "Consider it pro bono. It's a busy day for that. But thank Frank. He solved the case."

I rubbed my shoulder after Badger set me free. "Let's just get back to camp. I'm tired."

Doc took my arm. "Hold on, partner, you need to make a visit to the ER. I don't want you going septic on us. You'll end up hiring Daniel to sue me."

"No more pro bono work!" Daniel said, wagging his finger at us.
"My goodness," Miranda said, "you people are crazy."

Chapter Twelve

A false witness that speaketh lies, and he that soweth discord among brethren … Proverbs 6:19

Hundreds of bodies littered the fields like some bizarre interpretation of Dante's Inferno, the smoke and the stench of gunpowder drifting through the morning air, adding to the vision of Hell. Moans and cries of agony from the wounded and dying mingled with the constant cacophony of gunfire and the rumble of cannon. The morning of September 17th , in the year of 1862, had dawned with fear and expectation, and in a few hours had turned into the bloodiest day in American history. Captain Howard Long gathered his men into a skirmish line to advance once more toward the West Woods. His orders sounded hollow, a tiny voice in a churning ocean. Behind them, on the hills, sat the cannon of Stuart's horse artillery. They sent repeated volleys over the woods into the Union troops in Miller's cornfield.

To the south lay Sharpsburg, just past the little white church on the other side of the woods.

The 13th Virginia Regiment advanced through the West Woods in their skirmish lines, pushing the Union forces back.

"Mr. Long!"

Captain Long heard the call, but it sounded miles away. He glanced around to see if orders were coming down the line. What he saw was one man in filthy gray wool lying among the bodies. His hand, covered with dirt and blood, reached up imploringly, a drowning man clutching for a lifeline. The bright red of his blood contrasted sharply with the grime covering his skin. When Long looked at the face, he saw the pallor of the skin beneath the dirt that stained the man's face. The front of his shell jacket was ripped open, torn from Minié balls and covered with blood that soaked through the gray wool.

The soldier wasn't from the 13th, though his face looked familiar.

Long motioned Private McGinnis to follow him over to the man. They crouched down and Long uncorked his canteen. With one hand cradling the man's head, he lifted him slightly and lowered the canteen to his cracked lips.

"Owen," McGinnis said, surprised.

Long glanced from one to the other.

"It's Ben Owen," McGinnis said, pointing down at the wounded man. "Used to work at the general store in Ramsey. Hadn't seen him since we joined up."

Long studied the thin, filthy face. Yes, it was young Ben Owen. At least fifty pounds thinner, looking much older than his eighteen years, but then they all looked like walking skeletons. It was hard to even recognize his own face in the mirror when he shaved each morning. They were all starved, filthy, and exhausted.

"Hold steady, Mr. Owen," Long said as he shoved the cork back into the mouth of the canteen. "We'll get you to one of the field surgeons. They'll take care of you."

Owen licked a drop of water from his lips and shook his head. His voice was weak, barely more than a hoarse whisper. "No, sir. I ain't going to make it much longer."

Long patted his shoulder but avoided the gaping wound in Owen's stomach. They all knew the chances of surviving a gut wound. No telling what the ball had ripped apart on its way through, but from the looks of it, the damage was severe. There was so much blood and the smell was already nauseating. But Long had to give the man a little bit of false hope. He had heard of miracles happening and men surviving terrible wounds.

"We'll let the doctors and the Lord decide that one, Mister," Long said. "You just hang on and pray. We'll get you behind the lines to the surgeons. Just hang on. Don't be giving up."

Bloodstained fingers clutched his arm, making red streaks across the sleeve of his jacket.

"Naw, Mr. Long. I'm dead. They'd done killed me, sir." He swallowed hard, mustering his strength. "But I ain't prepared to go 'til I confess."

Owen must have been delirious.

"Mr. Owen, I am not a preacher and I don't know where our chaplain is at the moment. Let's get you behind the lines and the surgeons will find a chaplain for you."

Owen shook his head more adamantly. "No. It's you I gotta confess to, Mr. Long. It's you that's been wronged."

The wave of gunfire sounded closer. His men, crouching in their skirmish line, awaited his return. He couldn't afford to take this time and he couldn't really spare the men it would take to carry Owen up the hill to General Stuart's line of cannon. Besides, the man would be dead by the time they left the woods.

"Owen, I will send for a surgeon. Then we can talk later."

"There's no later. Not for me, Mr. Long."

Long tried to pry the fingers from his sleeve. They were slick and tacky. "I must return to my men, Mr. Owen. I will come back for you."

"It'll be too late. Please listen, sir. You was blamed for a train raid, but it weren't your fault."

Long stared down at the man and wondered what he was talking about. He had led the militia from Ramsey on a few train raids before they mustered into the Army of Northern Virginia, but that had been at the beginning of the war and mostly to stop supplies from travelling west.

Owen went on, gaining a little strength for one last surge. "Mr. Merryweather talked us into it. I worked in his general store. And some others worked the farms around the town. Those of us who hadn't joined up. He got us some old Confederate uniforms, pretty much rags, thrown out from the field hospital. But he gave us those fancy breech loaders to use. Must have stole them from a shipment going to the west. Stole or done some wily trading. Wish I had one of them Sharps here. Might have been different, instead of using that old Enfield. Mr. Merryweather, he led us north of town, and we robbed a train. Had a strongbox going to troops out west. He shot the officer, blowed his head clear off. Then we all started shooting. Killed the Federals. But they'd already surrendered, dropped their weapons. That just wasn't right, but Mr. Merryweather, he didn't want no witnesses. That officer knew him, had been in Ramsey when it was occupied, knew he owned the general store. Then Mr. Merryweather spread the word that you was the one who killed them all and stole the money, even though you wasn't around no more. We took that box back to town, and he hid it. He paid us each twenty dollars and promised a part of what we stole, but we never got none. But twenty dollars was still a lot of money, till it was all spent. Still nothing can get rid of what we'd done. It just weren't right, especially to you and your men. We ruined your good name, Mr. Long. I'm dreadful sorry. I don't want to die with this on me. I wanted you to know the truth."

The call came down the ranks and the 13th was on the move.

"We must go, Mr. Owen," Long said. He climbed to his feet and motioned to McGinnis to fall back into position. "We will return for you."

"It'll be too late. But it's all right, as long as you know. I'd done made my peace with you and the Lord. He done brought you here, so I could confess. Go, sir, and leave me here. It's all right, now."

Long could do no more for the man. He tried to put Owen out of his mind for now as he returned to his men. If someone did not come to his assistance, Long would return to him as he promised. He would do what he could, if it was only to comfort the fevered mind of the dying soldier.

He led his company through the West Woods toward the encroaching Federal troops. By the end of the day thousands were dead and Ben Owen was numbered among them. He never saw Owen again, alive or dead. He never had the opportunity. The army retreated over the Potomac and they were miles away before Long even thought about Owen and his delusional rambling. Or was it delusion?

*****

Ramsey had changed. War did that to a small town whose young men were taken away from it. The occasional Union occupation, with looting and destruction, had brought it further into despair. Many of the people had fled, especially when their farms were ravaged and their animals stolen and butchered. They had nothing left. The few who had remained clung to a little hope. Howard Long's farm had escaped destruction, but he had no more livestock and his corn had been devastated. The hand he had hired to care for the place had left. His wife, after his own insistence, had moved in with a cousin in Richmond. Long had just come from there, after a few weeks of recuperation from a wound to the leg, courtesy of a Federal soldier near Chancellorsville. Fortunately, the ball had not hit bone. The ball had been removed and the wound sewn up with horsehair suture. The scar would be there forever, but he had been more fortunate than most. He was alive and on his way to return to duty with two good feet beneath him. He just had one thing to do before he joined what was left of his men in Winchester.

His farmhouse had not been burned down, as some neighbors' houses had, but it had been emptied of anything remotely of value that his wife had not been able to take with her. Windows had been shattered and furniture smashed, and there was damage from the weather, but nothing that couldn't be repaired. It would take time, though, once this war was over.

His ride into Ramsey took him past the Ramsey's big house. On the porch, Mrs. Ramsey sat in a rocker, a black shrouded figure in mourning, waiting and watching for a husband who would never return. Long had not seen James Ramsey fall but had heard of it. He had been a likable man, but an ineffectual officer. His shattered body lay in a field near Chancellorsville. Where Major Ramsey had been a good man, his father had the opposite reputation. Long had never met him but had heard the stories of his drunkenness and the abuse of his slaves. He had been spoiled by his father's wealth, and it had fortunately not carried on to his late son. The younger Ramsey had the disposition his grandfather was famous for—a good man, kind and generous to slave as well as free man. The town had been named after the grandfather as a testimony of his goodness more than his wealth. It shamed the town that his son had darkened the lineage. Their bright hope in the younger generation had died at Chancellorsville.

The small street running through Ramsey was a somber scene, with many women wearing black, veils draped over their faces.

He received some curious looks from people he passed. William Bottoms noticed the uniform first and was about to tip his hat, but then recognized Long and turned his face as though he had just bitten down on a lemon. Mrs. Hickens made the same sour expression before turning her back to him. Others gave him a wide berth as though he were a leper.

He tied off his horse and hobbled up to the dry goods store. The leg always pained him after a ride, no matter how long. Given time, the limp would not be as pronounced, but it would probably never completely go away.

Elijah Merryweather stood behind the counter, his fingers running down the scrawled columns of the ledger opened before him. He looked up and noticed Long coming through the doorway. Long would have been a silhouette against the brightness of day flooding through the doorway and windows, indistinguishable from any other customer. He might notice the tattered uniform, though, and believe him to be from one of the Confederate regiments now occupying the town. Merryweather was a tall, thin man, a heavy mustache obscuring his upper lip and a narrow face that looked haggard when the lines deepened with certain expressions. Those lines were shallow as he smiled at the potential customer. They deepened as the smile faded when recognition drew upon him. One corner of his mouth twitched.

"Mr. Long, how good to see you well."

Long found no sincerity in the words. "Good afternoon, Mr. Merryweather." He did not bother with pleasantries he did not feel.

"I understand there has been quite a battle in Pennsylvania. Your regiment wasn't involved, was it? Is your regiment stationed near here?"

"I am on my way to rejoin my unit in Winchester." He had heard news of the battle on Northern soil and the terrible losses on the side of the South. The 13th Virginia had not been along with the rest of the Army of Northern Virginia but had been assigned to guard a railroad depot in Winchester. He would soon rejoin them.

"I see you are a captain. Very commendable, sir. So, what brings you to my humble store?"

"Ben Owen," Long said.

Merryweather's mouth twitched again and what had remained of the smile vanished. "Who?"

"Ben Owen. He worked for you. We met up a while back, at Sharpsburg."

"Oh. Is he well?"

"He is dead, shot in the gut. But he told me a curious story."

Merryweather slid the ledger off the counter and into a drawer. His eyes darted around to rest upon an older woman examining some bolts of cloth on a table on the far side of the store. "Really? I'm so sorry to hear of his death. He had been a good worker, very helpful around here. I've had to do all the heavy work and the cleaning myself since he and the other young men joined up." He hung his head and shook it. "So young to die in such a way. This war is terrible."

"You aren't curious about what he told me?"

He looked up, his eyes steely. "I am certain it was a bawdy yarn. He was always coming up with such stories, always making things up. Not an educated boy, if you understand me. But a good worker, a strong pair of arms."

"I asked around before coming here," Long said. "I was in Richmond for a time, on medical leave. I wrote a number of letters. It seems the Federal occupation of the town did not go well."

"Not at all. I am still making repairs, and supplies are still hard to come by for the residents to make their own repairs to their businesses and homes. Poor Mrs. Downy's son was executed for stealing a chicken the Federals stole from Mr. Kennedy's farm after they burned it to the ground."

"I understand you had little difficulties," Long said.

Merryweather drew up straight and glared back in indignation. "I cooperated. If you are suggesting anything more than that, you are mistaken. I had a business to run and a family to care for. I did what was told of me and put up no resistance. If I had not cooperated I would have been imprisoned or hung, and the Federals would have taken whatever they wanted."

"One thing they wanted was information," Long said, "about a train raid up north where their fellows were killed after being disarmed. They did not take kindly to that."

Merryweather's mouth drew into a tight line.

"I understand," Long went on, "that the occupying commander's own brother was among those killed. He took it upon himself to discover the circumstances of his brother's death and who was responsible. Was he satisfied with what he learned?"

Merryweather walked around the counter. "I am not privy to what a Union general thinks," he said. "Excuse me, Mr. Long. I do have customers." He headed across the store, but the woman examining the cloth had decided against a purchase and was casually walking out the door. Merryweather stopped, his back to Long, and paused as though he did not want to turn and face his unwanted guest.

Then he spun suddenly. "I have chores I must do, if you do not mind. As you know, I am without a helper and must do everything myself. Please excuse me, sir."

"What happened to the money, Mr. Merryweather?" Long asked.

Merryweather stopped short, then walked briskly to the wall behind the counter and snatched up a broom. "I have work I must do."

"Ben Owen and some other boys helped you to rob the train. You supplied some old gray uniforms and made it look like a Confederate raid. You had some breech loaders for them to use, to make quick work of the enemy. Maybe you didn't intended to do murder, but the Union officer knew who you were. You killed him, then the other men. Witnesses on the train only knew you as Confederates. What was in the strongbox you stole? Was it gold or Federal dollars? Either way, you have it hidden away. All you have to do is survive the war, then you will be rich. What was your profit, Mr. Merryweather?"

He stabbed the broom handle toward Long. "You don't know what you are talking about."

"Then educate me, sir."

"These are all lies. You take this story from a dead youth of unreliable heritage over what I say?"

"When the Union troops occupied Ramsey, your shop was not commandeered but you were left in business. I understand that you visited the Union general and that he put a bounty on my men and myself, which does not bother me since we are at war. I suspect that was your doing, blaming my men and I for that atrocity. I suspect that if any of us are ever captured, we might be tried and hung. I doubt the Federals would listen to my defense and surrender to reason. You see, it was impossible for us to perform that particular raid. We were stationed in Harper's Ferry at that time. But that had not been mentioned to the general, so he believed your story."

Merryweather stepped closer and glared down at Long, his jaw tight with rage. "You will leave my shop, Mr. Long. You are not wanted on these premises."

"From the looks I received when I rode into town, I see that some of my neighbors also believe your story. What will they think of you when they learn the truth?"

"Do not make baseless accusations, sir. I am well-respected in this community."

"We shall see," Long said and turned toward the door.

"Captain Long," Merryweather called before he left. "Do be careful when you return to your regiment. I understand that this war has taken a terrible toll on our young men in a great many ways. In battle, from illness, even due to friendly fire. Death can come from many directions." His voice was ice.

Long looked back. "Are you making a threat, sir?"

"Perish the thought," Merryweather said with a devilish grin. "Just a warning, sir. Have a good day."

Long turned and limped out of the store, never to see Merryweather or the town of Ramsey again, to die in battle from a Confederate bullet.

Chapter Thirteen

If we say that we have no sin, we deceive ourselves, and the truth is not in us ... 1st John 1:8

When Steve, Doc and I finally returned to camp, the regiment was settled down for the night. A few campfires still burned and some companies chatted in hushed tones. Lamps speckled the dark, occasionally one hovering over the field like an orb as someone carried a lantern on their way to the privy. Each member of our little company sat around the fire pit, taking in its warm, clinging to its light.

Jake popped up from his camp chair. "Everything okay?" He nodded toward my side and my ruined shirt.

"No problem," I said. I wasn't feeling anything at the moment due to the local anesthetic. Tomorrow would be a different matter, especially after sleeping on a bed of straw. As per Doc's prediction, I did have a few stitches. With the torn shirt still stained with blood I looked like a battle casualty. It would have to be my best shirt.

Steve dragged our camp chairs nearer to the fire and I sat between Badger and Jake, while Steve headed toward our tent.

Badger shook his head. "What you go and do that for, Frank? Red could've killed you. He's pretty nasty with that blade of his. Not as quick as he used to be, but he's still got a rep."

"I didn't expect anything like that," I said, "not from him. I was more worried about that big guy, Diablo." To me, Red was just a drunken, middle-aged, overweight biker. And not very bright. I hadn't given him much thought. How was I to know his temper snapped so easily and he liked to poke people with a knife?

I eased myself into the chair. Boy, I was tired. "Thanks for showing up tonight, Cap'n," I said to Jake.

He shrugged. "I take care of my men," he said in a mock voice of a macho commander. "Daniel called me, and we got as many guys together as we could on such short notice and rushed over."

"Hey," Daniel said, throwing up his hands, "I wasn't about to go in there without back-up. I'm a lawyer, not an idiot."

"So I'm an idiot," I said after a brief bit of deductive reasoning.

Daniel pointed at me. "At least you're admitting to it. Heck, you were mad. I've never seen you that angry. I guess if I was that upset I wouldn't have thought reasonably either."

Badger grunted. "Well, if he don't call you an idiot, I will. That was one big stupid thing you did. Even without Red trying to stick you, or Diablo about to pound you, any of those creeps in there would have taken you apart just for looking at them wrong. And then talking to Jewel the way you done, you'd be lucky to get out alive. Those guys don't take kindly to anyone coming down on their own, especially on a woman. They'll dish out any kind of abuse and threats, but they won't take any. What you grinning at?"

"You," I said, laughing. "Did you notice how you were referring to the people in the bar?"

His heavy brow furrowed. "How?"

"Red could have killed you."

"Third person," I said. "Like you aren't including yourself among them."

He grunted again. "Now you're starting to sound like an English teacher." He folded his arms over his chest to end the discussion.

"He's right," Doc said. "You're not thinking of yourself as one of them anymore, Badger. I think you've finally put them behind you, separated yourself from the past."

"I ain't one of them," he snapped. "Fact is, I feel like I never was."

"Hey!"

I jumped up at the sound of Steve's voice. His cry had come along the lane of canvas tents. A number of other sounds followed his outburst, most notably one that suggested a heavy object falling to the ground.

I flew out of the chair and raced through the camp.

In the inadequate glow of a lantern hanging on a pole outside one of the nearby tents I saw Steve roll over the ground and struggle to get up. A large shadow stood over him and for a moment I thought of the enigmatic Union colonel with his cryptic warnings. But then I saw the beam of a flashlight inside our tent, turning the canvas into a glowing haze and showing off a skulking shadow inside the tent. The beam flashed onto the ground outside the tent as the flaps flew open and the shadow stuck his head out.

The beam dashed over the man outside, illuminating the huge biker. He pulled his foot back, about to send the pointed toe of his boot into Steve's side.

Without slowing down, I hurled myself at him.

It was like hitting a steel-reinforced brick wall.

With one foot up, swinging back, Diablo was off balance. When I hit him, he wobbled, then toppled. We crashed to the ground and I felt a stitch in my side give way. Pain shot through me, despite the medication. As I lay on top of his broad back, I wondered what I was going to do next. It was like jumping onto the back of a wild tiger. But Diablo took that matter into his own hands by twisting and slamming one arm against me, hurtling me from him. Pain exploded through my side. Hands grabbed hold of me and I struggled, but they were only there to help me to my feet. Doc and Jake pulled me up just as Diablo jumped to his feet.

Diablo's skinny companion stepped out of our tent, his flashlight beam playing over everyone in the lane.

Badger had his arms around Steve, helping to steady him. He turned an angry glare at Diablo.

"What're you doing here!?"

Diablo's broad grin appeared forced. "See you got sprung, eh, *amigo*?"

In reply, Badger stepped into Diablo with a swing that would have broken bones on a smaller man. The big biker stumbled back into his friend. He worked his jaw, wiped blood from his chin, then spat blood and a tooth onto the ground.

"I said," Badger continued tightly, "what are you doing here?"

For a moment Diablo looked as though he would launch himself at Badger. I stepped up beside Badger, ready to interfere. Jake came up on the other side. Steve, rubbing his arm, stepped to my side. Then Doc, Daniel, Sam and Charlie crowded in. Sam had his bayonet and was slapping it against his palm.

Diablo laughed and spat again.

"What you going to do, Badger? Gang up on us? Goin' to shoot us with your muskets?"

"You know what I can do," Badger said calmly, and Diablo lost his grin.

"I want that book," Diablo said. "Just let me have it, and there ain't no more trouble."

"What book?" Badger asked. "You can't even read."

The skinny biker snarled. "Can too."

Diablo slapped him across his chest and he fell sullen. "That old book the kid had," Diablo explained. "Some *gringo* paid me to get it."

"The journal," Steve said. "Captain Long's journal."

We each looked at each other. "You mean," Doc said, "the one you and the young lady had at the sheriff's office? Who would want that? Who knew about it?"

Steve shrugged. "But I don't have it. Jenna does. She took it home with her. And the only one I know who wanted it bad enough is her grandfather, Mr. Merryweather."

"Did Merryweather pay you?" Badger asked.

Diablo threw up his hands in impatience. "I don't know, man. Old white guy, with gray hair and beard. Don't know him from jack. Just paid me fifty, said there was another when I bring it back."

The other biker grabbed Diablo's thick arm. "C'mon, man, they ain't got it. Let's ride."

Diablo shook his arm to toss off the other man's fingers. "Shut up, Slick. I'll handle it." Then he turned on Badger. "Look, *amigo*, no problem. You ain't got it, it's okay. We tossed the kid's tent and it weren't there. Okay, we'll leave, no sweat." He raised his hands to show he meant no harm, then started backing away.

I heard some tiny electronic beeping and turned to see what was making the noise. Daniel had his cell phone out, punched in numbers, and held it to his ear.

"I'd like to leave a message for Sheriff Ellis, please," he said into the phone. "This is Attorney Daniel Meyers."

Diablo stabbed his finger in Daniel's direction. "Hold on, man. I said we was leavin'. No need to get no sheriff. Hang up, man."

Daniel held the phone a few inches from his ear. "Well, we are just insuring that you don't wander back later. Or that you won't pay the young lady a visit. I suggest you pocket the fifty Mr. Merryweather gave you and ride out of town. Count yourself fortunate and fifty dollars richer. Right?"

Diablo shook his head. "Man, you is one uppity—"

"Don't!" I snapped, unaware that I had stepped toward the huge man.

The others had also stepped forward, as though we were all one indignant mass about to bowl over the hapless bikers. Slick discreetly backed away and vanished into the darkness, his flashlight beam bouncing over the ground. Daniel began talking with the sheriff's receptionist. The rest of us stared Diablo down.

He shrugged. "No problem, man. We was about to ride out anyway. Keep your freakin' book, kid. Doesn't mean nothing to me. I'm outta here."

He turned and walked away. After a few moments, Sam and Charlie followed at a safe distance. In about ten minutes, we heard the loud motors of two hogs rumbling down the highway in the distance.

"Why is Merryweather so obsessed with that journal?" Daniel asked.

"I read it," Steve said. "It totally destroys the article he wrote on the train raid when Ramsey's Raiders were blamed for murder. And it makes his ancestor, Elijah, into the murderer and thief. If Long's account is accurate, which I'm convinced it is, Elijah Merryweather was not only a Union collaborator, a black marketer and a traitor, but he planned the raid, murdered the Union soldiers, and hid the money. Jenna told me that after the war, he was able to buy up property and eventually start the local bank. He must have used that money, a little at a time so no one would notice. The journal even mentions threats to Long if he tried to expose Merryweather, and then Long was killed by friendly fire not long after. I'm guessing Elijah paid someone to do the job, to make sure Long never made the truth known. He just never knew about the journal. Now Jenna's grandfather wants to keep everything quiet, to save his reputation and his family name."

"Why would that matter much today?" Jake asked.

"Because," Daniel said, "our Mr. Merryweather will be shown as a liar, his articles inaccurate, and his inherited fortune based on theft and murder. It could destroy his reputation, at least in this community."

"Probably in the Civil War community, too, now I think about it" Jake said, nodding. "If his research is proved faulty, his reputation as a historian will be ruined. He'll find it hard to publish, if not impossible."

*****

The camp had settled down, and we were the only ones still up, huddled around the dying fire. Jake sipped on the last of the coffee. Sam nervously shuffled a deck of playing cards. Charlie puffed on a slim, elegant cigar. The general feeling was one of elation, but no one seemed ready to retire for what was left of the night. The crisis was over, we had a big day tomorrow with two battles and assorted events for the spectators, and we would be tearing down the camp and leaving for home by evening. We were all exhausted, but none of us were willing to leave and crawl into our respective tents. Conversation was at a minimum, punctuated by an occasional yawn.

Once in a while someone from one of the other units would wander by on the way to the port-a-potties lined up at a respectable distance from the tents. Usually they carried a lantern or a flashlight. No one thought it was unusual for a man to be standing near our little group, but I for one couldn't remember seeing him approach. He walked quietly around our circle, the light from the fire playing across his blue uniform and slouch hat, lighting up his pale face and drooping mustache. The colonel straps on his shoulders were still in shadows.

Jake's head popped up and followed him, then Daniel's. Badger's brow furrowed with suspicion, then relaxed slightly as he took in the uniform.

"Mind if I join you, boys?" the colonel asked as he took an empty camp chair between Jake and me.

"Suit yourself," Jake said.

I stared at Jake, then the colonel. The man looked real—substantial, a three-dimensional solid. The fire glowed over him just as it did the rest of us. And the others could see him. I was not hallucinating. He couldn't be a ghost. I refrained from poking him with a finger, but I knew that I would feel the rough wool of his sack coat and his solid body underneath. I found myself smiling. Maybe I wasn't going insane.

"Can we do something for you?" Doc asked. "We're all out of coffee."

The colonel leaned back and folded his arms around himself. "We will meet on the battlefield tomorrow," he said.

"Yeah, right," Jake said. "And we'll whip your butts, twice over. We got two battles tomorrow, just like today."

"We shall meet on the field of honor to extract retribution for the atrocities you have perpetrated," the colonel said.

"That's what you said last night at the Ramsey Mansion," I said. "Mind making it clearer for us?"

He turned toward me. The dying fire cast a red glow over his face, but his eyes refused to catch the light and reflect it. They were like twin pits of blackness. "I am here to take vengeance for the murders of the brave soldiers killed in the train raid. You will all pay for the atrocity, just as the others have paid."

Each of the others had expressions of confusion, except Badger, who studied the colonel with furrowed brows over eyes burning with hatred. Steve's jaw hung slack for a moment until he swallowed uncomfortably.

"Do you mean," Daniel said, "the way all the men from the original company died before the end of the war?"

"Yes," the colonel said.

"Well, now, that just don't make sense," Badger said. "We weren't there."

"Nevertheless, we shall meet on the field of honor."

Out of the corner of my eyes I saw a flash of red. Steve was on the other side of the fire pit, next to Badger, and something silver glittered in his hands. He was fidgeting with it. The red flashed again, and I saw a red thread of light stab through the smoke billowing up from the burning logs.

"It's a lie anyway," Steve said, his voice quivering. "Long … Captain Long wasn't involved in that raid. I read his journal today, in his own handwriting. His men had nothing to do with that one, when the Union soldiers were killed. He … his company was already with the regular army by then." His voice grew stronger, more confident. "It was some people from the town. One guy confessed to Long before he died. It was all the idea of Mr. Merryweather's ancestor, Elijah Merryweather. He's the one who killed the soldiers from the train, making it look like Confederate soldiers did it. Your whole story is a lie."

The red string of light danced through the smoke from Steve's laser pointer. I saw the dot strike Jake and slide across his green homespun shirt, flash off the brass fitting on his suspenders, then move away. It hit the dirty canvas wall of the tent behind us, then vanished. It reappeared in a moment after a gap of about two feet. It played across my shirt, then it started its journey back toward Jake.

Each of us were watching it now. The beam did not move across the blue sack coat of the colonel.

Badger stood up suddenly, his rage bursting free. "I know what you are! I thought so before, but I'm sure now. You ain't here for vengeance or any of that crap. You're straight from the devil, and I'll send you right back."

The colonel smiled, and there was no sense of humor or warmth in the expression. "And I know you, Graham Price. I know the things you have done in your past. I know the times you stole, the times you used drugs, even the people you assaulted and the women you abused. We were there every time. You are hardly so pure and innocent to make accusations to others."

Badger's mouth hung open. He dropped back into his chair, falling like a balloon deflating.

"And I know you, John Boden," he said as he turned to Jake. "I know the reason you would not enter the military. I know why your wife divorced you. Shall I tell your companions about your fear, your cowardice? You have a life without accomplishments, a life filled with failures, a life filled with regrets. Can you honestly be the leader of these men?"

Jake turned his face away from the colonel and hung his head.

"Terrance Carmine," the colonel went on, "how many people did you kill?"

"That was war, mister," Doc snapped.

"You have seen death, but you cringe at the thought of your own. Do you want to see what awaits you on the other side?" The colonel smiled again, and ice ran up my spine.

"No!" Doc snapped.

The colonel turned his hollow gaze at Daniel. "Daniel Meyers, Attorney-at-law, who denies his heritage."

"I do not," Daniel shot back.

"You do. You have forsaken your people, your black heritage. You see the hate in their eyes, but you cannot accept it."

"No ..." Daniel began, but his voice faded away.

"Samuel Kruger," the colonel said. "How much money have you lost this weekend? You cannot live without playing the game and you cannot play the game without gambling. But you are not very good at playing. You lose more than you win, a lot more. How much do you owe? How much have you lost? Do not believe you will see your wife again. She is finished with you and your gambling. You love the game so much, love it more than you ever loved her."

"That's not true," Sam said, shaking his head. He sounded like he was trying to convince himself.

"And Charles Cooper," the colonel went on. "You love the ladies, do you not? And they love you. How can they not? You are tall, young, handsome. Any one of them is yours for the taking."

"But I haven't," Charlie protested. "I won't cheat on my wife."

"But you do so in your mind, Charles. I know, because we can see in there. We know your desires. But is it really women you want, or is it the feelings their admiration brings? You have fear, too, of losing that which attracts them. You fear growing old, maturing, losing your youth. You fear the responsibilities of marriage and family. And why not? Why should you waste your finest years with one woman? When you are old—that is when you should settle down, become stagnant. Not yet. Not while you can revel in adulation for your charm and good looks."

Then he turned slowly toward me and I felt myself falling into a black pit. "Frank Blaine. Why did you try to talk to that boy? What arrogance did you have that made you believe you could help? Instead, you made matters worse. You are not trained in psychology. You are a teacher, nothing more and probably less. You might as well have pulled that trigger yourself. Because of you—"

"Stop!" I heard Steve shout.

The blackness around me vanished.

Steve continued, "You weren't there. My dad tried to help that kid."

"Steve," I said weakly.

"Well, this guy's lying. I know you tried to help. Jeremy was just too far gone."

The colonel stood up. "You, Steven Blaine, face an uncertain future. You see many paths, but you cannot find the one that is best for you, where you will succeed. You are afraid to leave the comfort of your home and find the right path. Too many to choose from. You fear the loneliness, the world opening up to you, the decisions you must make. From now on you must choose your own path, instead of your father doing so for you. What path will you choose at dawn when we meet on the battlefield? What will each of you choose?"

Jake stood also. "We won't be meeting you, on the field or anywhere else."

The colonel nodded. "Just the response I would expect from a coward who pretends to be a leader. We shall meet, all of you, and each of you will face your defeat."

He walked away and was no longer there. He didn't vanish into the darkness surrounding the camp, he didn't fade away like smoke or vapor; it was more like he expanded and the night became a little darker.

Chapter Fourteen

In a dream, in a vision of the night, when deep sleep falleth upon men, in slumberings upon the bed ... Job 33:15

The dreams were always accurate, not twisted representations of reality. Sometimes they began in my classroom, as I prepared my notes for the day's lectures and labs. Sometimes I'm already in the boys' lavatory facing Jeremy with his gun already pointed at his temple. The lav was usually vague, like in my memories of the moment. If someone had said it happened in the gym, I would have taken their word for it. I just couldn't remember the details. Tonight, the tiled lavatory took on crisp clarity. The ancient stains, the broken latches on the stall doors, the chipped fixtures, the missing tiles, the holes in the ceiling tiles, the fresh graffiti, the grimy windows and the dead flies on the sills. Everything leaped out at me at once. At first I was alone, standing near the door to the hall. I should have heard kids in the hall, chattering in a soft storm punctuated by the bangs of lockers as they prepared for the morning classes. But there was nothing. I could have been utterly alone in the whole building. I felt a sense of detachment and decided that the lavatory itself could have been removed from the school and exist on its own plane in an empty universe. Had I turned and pushed open the door, I would have met a cold black void.

Jeremy stood against the far wall by the windows. I didn't bother to question his sudden appearance. After all, he belonged here. The bright morning sun should be bursting through the windows, casting him into a silhouette, but the lighting seemed to come from the rows of fluorescent bulbs overhead. Jeremy was as clear and detailed as the rest of the scene, from his scuffed Reeboks to his oversized jeans to his long tee shirt with the logo of some rock band. He was a thin boy, seventeen, with short hair of a neutral brown, acne, and wisps of facial hair. He was quiet, sat in the back of the classroom, kept to himself—a loner. He was one of those kids that was neither an overachiever nor a troublemaker, so he got lost in the cracks. He became almost invisible.

Except in the boys' lav that day.

"This isn't a good idea, Jeremy," I said. Just like I had when I came slowly into the lav to find him in the empty room, the silhouette of the gun in his hand. It may have been a toy gun for all I knew then, but now in this strange clarity I saw every detail of its burnished metal.

"I don't want to hurt you, Mr. Blaine."

His voice squeaked as it had then, with fear and the adrenaline rush. Sweat soaked his tee shirt and trickled down his temples.

"That's good," I said. "Is there someone you want to hurt?" I tried to sound casual, almost lighthearted while my chest pounded in terror.

"Yeah. A couple." His voice gathered some strength.

"Who?"

"Mrs. Wilson for one. And Mr. Hines. They're the ones."

"Why?"

"Because they're failing me, dude. Ah, Mr. Blaine. They're failing me, and I can't graduate. I gotta go to summer school. I can't do that."

"You'll graduate, just after you make up those classes. No big deal, Jeremy. It happens every year. Besides, you won't be by yourself. At least ten kids are in the same boat. It's no problem."

"Yes it is. My dad …"

"What about your dad?"

"Nothing!" He shouted and swung the gun towards me.

I threw up my hands and took a step back. "Hold on, Jeremy, hold on. Take it easy."

"No! I'm like a nobody here. Everybody ignores me. *They* ignore me. Except when I screw up, then everything comes down on me. I'm not gonna fail. I'm not gonna take summer school. I need to graduate, now."

"Calm down, Jeremy. Have you talked to your counselor about this? Maybe he could talk to your teachers, talk to your parents." He shoved the gun through the air at me and I expected to hear it explode.

"That creep? Caruthers? He's a useless piece of crap, like most of the staff here. He doesn't care anything except when he can retire. What do you think he'd do? Get a parent/teacher conference so they can decide what's best for me? No way, man! They'll tell my dad how lousy I am in their classes, then he grounds me, takes the car from me, makes me quit my job. No way. I need that job. I need to get outta here."

"And you think by threatening teachers you'll be okay?" I asked. "Everything will be fine then?"

He looked at the gun, turned it slowly in front of his red-rimmed eyes, as if seeing it for the first time and suddenly understanding a revelation of why it was in his hand. A slow smile parted his dry lips.

"Yeah," he said slowly. "Everything'll be fine, then."

He started towards me, toward the doorway I blocked, but I held up my hands. "Jeremy, I can't let you go out there. I can't let you go into the halls with that gun. Just give it to me, and we can both go out. No problem." What would happen after that was anyone's guess, but I had to get the gun away from him. Obviously, the police would be brought in. Charges might be filed. He'd be in a lot more trouble with his parents than with just failing a couple of classes and being condemned to summer school. But he could not go into the halls with that gun. Visions of him opening up on teachers and students flashed through my mind. My own son was out there, in his own homeroom. Jeremy was not leaving with that gun.

"No!" he snapped.

"Look," I said, trying to calm the thundering heart that threatened to burst through my chest cavity. "You know I can't let you out there. You can't threaten teachers with that gun. You won't accomplish anything and you'll scare the heck out of the other kids. Do you want that?"

"What do I care? They never cared about me. They couldn't care less about me. As if I had any friends here. They're all a bunch of jerks."

"But they aren't the problem, Jeremy. And failing a couple classes isn't the problem, is it?"

He thought for a moment. "Sure it is. If I wasn't failing, I wouldn't get into trouble. Everything would be fine."

I had heard the horror stories about abusive parents. Every teacher has, and we have been warned to watch for the warning signs. How could I broach the subject, get him to explain what his father did to him? I wasn't trained in this area, but he had no respect for the school counselor. At the moment I doubted he had any respect for any adult, even me.

"What will your father do to you?"

"Huh? I told you, he'd ground me. He'd make me quit my job, or do something stupid that'll make them fire me."

"Nothing ... physical?"

"You think he beats me? He doesn't care enough to raise a finger. He just doesn't want to look stupid. He doesn't care what I do, except fail. He don't want a failure for a son. I've heard that like a million times. I can't make him look bad."

"And what about you? How does this make you look?" I pointed toward the gun.

"I don't care."

"You'd better. You'll end up in jail, Jeremy. Juvenile hall. You'll lose your job that way. Stick it out for a few months, and you'll be old enough to move out on your own."

He gave a gruff laugh. "Like I'd be able to without a job."

"Get another one. Join the army. Anything's better than going to jail. You walk out that door with that gun and you'll be making the biggest mistake you'd ever make. It's your whole life I'm talking about, Jeremy. Don't ruin it now. Give me the gun and maybe we can keep this all quiet. Go out there, and it'll never be erased."

"Yeah, it's my life. Nobody seems to think about that. It's always been about my dad. Don't ruin it for him, don't make him look stupid. Don't make waves. Keep quiet, keep outta the way, keep outta my face. No one cares about me, no one ever did, I'm just one big pain, not good for anything, a failure. I'm just a failure. I even suck at this, man."

He raised the gun up.

"No!"

My scream evaporated under the explosion of the gun.

In the moment before the flash, Jeremy's face faded and Steve was standing there, the barrel of the gun pressed against his own temple, his blue eyes looking at me with that same hopelessness. Then the blast obscured his features in a cloud of fire that sprayed out blood and brains and fragments of skull. The gory mass peppered the tiled wall, the stained mirrors, the chipped sinks.

I couldn't hear the body drop to the grimy floor. I couldn't hear anything except the thunderous blast echoing over and over in my ears.

Chapter Fifteen

And the seventh angel poured out his vial into the air; and there came a great voice out of the temple of heaven, from the throne, saying, It is done ... Revelation 16:17

I woke up with a start, already sitting straight up.

Steve flicked on the small flashlight we kept on a stool for nighttime emergencies and excursions to the privy. He flashed it across my face and I squeezed my eyes shut, spots dancing on the inside of my lids.

"You okay?" he asked.

I nodded, not yet trusting my voice.

The light moved away, and I blinked away the afterflash while Steve fumbled around, the flashlight beam rolling over the canvas of the tent. In a moment a match flared and Steve lit the candle inside our lantern. The expanse of our tent filled with the warm glow.

Steve sat for a while watching me. I could hear someone else moving around the camp, probably someone on his way to visit the privy.

"That dream again?" he asked.

I wasn't aware he knew about the dreams.

"It wasn't your fault, Dad."

"I don't want to talk about it."

"I think you should. Y'know, you can help other people talk out their problems, but you won't do the same for yourself. Jeremy killed himself. You didn't do it. You didn't talk him into it."

"I didn't talk him out of it. I didn't get the gun from him."

"Nope. You probably couldn't. He brought it there to use, whether on himself or someone else. There wasn't anything you could do, Dad. Y'know, if you hadn't kept him in the lav, he might've shot someone else. I know a couple kids that picked on him, so he probably hated them. He would have gone after them."

"Maybe. He told me he was upset at two teachers for failing him."

"See?"

"But I was close," I said. I pushed off the blanket and gum blanket and sat up on my knees. "I know I was close. I almost had him talked out of it. Just a few more minutes—"

"Dad. You're a science teacher. A biologist. You're not a psychologist."

"But I could have stopped him …"

"No. Actually, Jeremy was nuts. He had problems. There wasn't anything you could have done. Not for him. You stopped anyone else from getting hurt. I think that's pretty great."

I looked at him in the lantern's glow. "Yeah?"

"Yeah. That must have been pretty awful. I mean, for you to be there."

"I never thought of that."

After a while, he asked, "Do you keep seeing it? I mean, that's what the dreams are, isn't it? Do you keep replaying it?"

"Yeah. Sometimes it's different, like …" The image of Steve's face exploding flashed through my mind. I grimaced at the image, at remembering his blue eyes the moment the gun went off.

"What?" he asked.

"Well, ah, it was you."

"Me?"

"Ah . . . yeah."

"You think I'd do something like that? Dad, just because I got problems occasionally, that I get depressed sometimes, doesn't mean I'd use a gun. I'm not like Jeremy. He had some big problems. Besides that, his parents didn't care. They weren't involved with him, didn't do anything with him. He had no friends, had no family. No way is that like me. I got you and Mom. And I got my faith in God. I got problems. Everybody has problems. Just look at the guys here."

"Yeah, right," I said, smiling.

"Don't worry about me, Dad."

"I will. It's my job."

I heard more scuffling outside. More than one person was out and about, and they weren't just taking a trip to the port-a-potty. It was still dark outside, and it felt like we had just gone to sleep, so it couldn't be morning already. When Steve dug out his pocket watch and told me it was almost five, I groaned. But who was moving around camp this early? We weren't scheduled for a dawn battle reenactment.

"What's going on out there?" I scrambled toward the tent flap.

Daniel crawled out of his tent at the same time. He blinked at me from behind his glasses. Together we looked around the camp to see the dark shapes moving about. For a moment I thought I was seeing apparitions again, more things I couldn't explain. Was I still going crazy? Everyone in the company had seen the Union colonel. And we saw Steve's laser light pass right through him. I couldn't tell what he was, or what the other things I had seen were. Now they were taking over the camp. At least, I thought so until Jake passed into the circle of light from a lantern burning low on a peg under the fly. And one squat shape I recognized as Doc. Did everyone have insomnia?

"What's going on?" Daniel asked.

I shrugged. "That's what I was wondering. Couldn't you sleep?"

Steve ducked out of the tent after me, and we walked toward the fly. Badger's huge bulk stood over the smoldering fire. He poked at it, stirring up some of the embers. Around us the tents were all silent, the expanse of the Confederate Army's camp lost in a darkness blanketed in a low, thick mist. No one was about except for our company. The quiet was almost oppressive—not even a chirp from an insect.

"I was fast asleep," Daniel said, "until a few minutes ago. I had some weird dream, then all of a sudden I was awake. I'm wide-awake now. You?"

"Nightmare," I said. I wondered what sort of dream had gotten him awake, after considering my own dream. What could be bothering him?

"What's everyone up for?" Doc's hushed voice called. "Can't anyone sleep around here? I hope it wasn't dinner taking revenge." He tried to laugh but stifled it when it sounded eerie in the cool night.

"We were wondering that, too," I said. "Jake? Badger? Any of you guys have weird dreams? Is that what got you up?"

Badger poked at the charred logs and grunted. Whether that was a yes or no, I couldn't tell. Jake, though, began nodding. Doc nodded too, though more slowly.

"Yeah," Jake said. "I dreamt I was in a war. A real one. A modern one, in some endless desert. Bombs exploding all over the place. Jets strafing the ground. I couldn't see the enemy. I was in the front lines but I didn't have any weapon. I was supposed to lead troops, but no one would listen to me."

"That was a darn sight better than mine," Daniel said. "I dreamt I was a slave. Man, it was nasty. All those terrible stories we've ever heard, I went through them. Beatings, hard labor, starvation. Then I was about to be hung for running away. That's when I woke up. It was pretty awful. My back even hurts where I was whipped."

"That's terrible," I said. "Daniel, those things happened. What we do doesn't condone it, you know that."

"Yeah," he said weakly.

Sam hung his head and kicked at the dust. Something prompted me to question him. "My dream was about my wife, the day she walked out. I haven't seen her for weeks. It all played out again. Not like a dream, like I was living it all over again."

I put my hand on his shoulder and he sniffed, then wiped his knuckle across his nose.

"Doc?" I said, turning to him.

He shook his head. "Frank, y'know I've seen more'n my share of death. It ain't pretty no matter what, and I have nightmares just about every night. Tonight was different. Tonight I saw myself dead. It was weird. I can remember being in the jungle. I could even smell the rot and the mud. I'd come up on a casualty, and it'd be me. Then I was riding the ambulance to a car accident, and I'd be the one lying on the highway in the middle of the wreck. I—What about you? Did you see that kid?"

I shrugged and tried to sound casual. "Nothing new about that."

Charlie slowly walked up to us, his hair and clothes immaculate like he hadn't even lain down. "Me too," he said. "Had a dream, that is. I dreamt I was old. Not just fifty, sixty—no offense, Doc. But I looked like something from The Mummy. Or Dorian Gray's portrait. Everyone around me, young women mostly, they were all laughing at me. I was a decrepit thing no one wanted anything to do with."

Badger poked at the logs again, stirring up a few embers. One sliver of a log crumbled into a pile of ashes. He hadn't joined in our little cluster and he obviously had something bothering him. I left the others under the fly and stood over his crouched form.

"What about you, Badger? Everyone seems to have had a weird dream. You heard us all. What about you?"

He shook his head.

"You dreamt about your past, didn't you? When you rode with the Warriors. Listen, Badger, all that's past. You said yourself, the old man's dead, you're a new creation."

He stood up and towered over me. "Man, you don't know. You don't know what I was like. I can't run away from it."

"Are you supposed to?" I asked.

"Huh?" He stared at me, his face in the shadows of the night. He stood up, like a leviathan rising from the deep.

"We can't erase what we've done." I glanced over my shoulder and raised my voice a little to catch everyone's attention. "We can't change what we've done, no matter what it was. We learn from it and move on, try to become a better person."

"Easy for you to say, Frank," Badger said with a trace of a sneer in his voice.

"No. No it isn't. I watched a kid blow his brains out, and I know, I just know, there was something I could have said, or done, to stop it. Every night I see him do it, again and again, and I try to rewrite what I told him, and I wonder if something I said triggered him into shooting himself. I have to live with that, Badger."

I realized that the others had gathered around me.

"That's different from me, Frank," Badger insisted, less hostile.

"What, God can't forgive you?" I asked, wondering if I had bothered to ask forgiveness for my own shortcomings.

"Of course he can!"

"Then trust Him," I said. "He forgave you, He's taken care of it, He has other things for you to do."

"Like what?" he asked with a sarcastic edge. "I'm just an old biker."

"You don't know what I was like."

"You're the company chaplain," Jake said.

"Yeah," Steve said.

"Right," Doc said.

The others bobbed their heads.

Badger shook his. "You guys are sick. Me? Chaplain?"

Assent echoed among us. "None of us knows more about the Bible than you, Badger," Doc pointed out. "Can't say I've heard you preach, but we've sure had some lively talks around the camp. You know your stuff. 'Course, Chaplain Badger doesn't have a good godly ring to it. How's Chaplain Graham Price sound?"

"Who's that?" Steve asked.

Badger grunted a rough chuckle. "Me. My real name. Not too rough sounding for riding a hog. Haven't used it since I ran away from home, but it sounds better than my old handle."

"Since Badger's now the company's chaplain," Steve said, bouncing on his heels, "can I be first sergeant?"

"No!" Jake said quickly, echoed by Doc.

"Okay, okay," Daniel said, holding up his hands. "This is nice, but what about what got us all up in the first place. Do any of you think that it is a little strange we all had nightmares, or at the least weird dreams?"

Badger grunted. "Yeah. It's all his doing." He nodded out into the mist-shrouded darkness.

"Who?" I asked.

He gazed at me evenly. "You should know, Frank. You're the one who's been seeing him all weekend. He's been playin' with your head, making you crazy, making you think there were ghosts. Weren't no ghosts, Frank, just him and his cohorts. There ain't no such thing as ghosts, and we saw him just as you did, so there's only one answer. And now he's playing with all our heads. I ain't saying he's Satan, but he's a devil and he's calling us out."

This wasn't much better than the other alternatives. Maybe Badger slipped his mental gears. Maybe my mind had snapped and I was actually still in my bedroll and everyone else was really asleep in their own tents. "You mean demons? I've been seeing demons?" The mental picture I had of twisted little gargoyles didn't fit with the colonel, Mrs. Ramsey, or any of the other apparitions of this weekend.

"Yep." Badger nodded and set his jaw. "And he's challenging us. I ain't saying he's caused things to happen this weekend, like me seeing people I used to ride with, or all that with the old journal, but he's had his hands in it, manipulated things. Used the old train raid to fool us. But that's not what he's after, retribution for the murders. That was a lie. He's challenging each of us and we've got to face him."

"Huh?" I stared at him. Great, I was so worried about my own sanity that I hadn't seen this coming. While I wondered how a half dozen men of roughly average size could restrain a grizzly bear, I turned to look at the others and was shocked to find them nodding in agreement.

Jake's own face was tight with determination. "What do we do, Badger?"

Badger motioned his head toward the old battlefield, in the general direction of the Union camp. The rolling hills and the scattering of trees lay between, now blanketed in night. "He's waiting for us. Remember what he said. We've got to meet him on the field. That's the only way we can defeat him and he'll leave us alone. He's out there with his own company, waiting."

"That's ridiculous," I said.

"No it isn't, Dad," Steve said. He was bouncing again. "He's right. In a way. That colonel used the train raid atrocity to hook us, but we know that it's historically inaccurate. Long's company wasn't responsible. But that isn't why he's here. He just used that to challenge us. We have to face him, show him we're not afraid of him, then we can chase him away. Right?"

Badger nodded. "Right. 'We wrestle not against flesh and blood ...' We march in there and show him we ain't afraid of him or his demons."

I held up my hands for them to move a little slower. "How about we go back to bed and ignore him. He can't do anything if we don't go out there."

"You can't ignore evil," Badger said. "It won't go away. It'll just keep getting stronger."

I put both hands over my eyes, pressing hard, then shook my head. When I brought my hands down, my friends had broken apart and were digging in their respective tents. They came out with shell jackets on, strapping leathers about them. Muskets were leaned against the tents so that the equipment could be buckled and adjusted. Kepis and slouch hats were set and rifles were taken up.

"C'mon, Dad," Steve said.

I turned to see him in uniform, musket held tight in both hands. "You are not going," I told him.

He looked hurt. "I have to." He looked around at the company. "Hey, I know these guys are way older than me, but they're my friends. I can't let them go without me. Besides, that colonel picked me out. He said I was afraid of the future. Well, I guess I am in a way. I'll be going to college in a few weeks. I don't know what's going to happen. It's a big change, and it does sort of scare me. I had a weird dream, too, Dad. I was in some strange place I've never seen before, surrounded by people I didn't know. But I guess the future's that way. We just don't know what's ahead."

I put my arm around his shoulders and thought of how he had changed from the toddler he was not so long ago. It was a big change for me, too, and he wasn't the only one scared. "I'm always there for you."

"What about now?" he asked.

I scowled at him, then ducked into our tent to dig out my own equipment. As I went to fall in line, I passed Doc's tent. His flap swung up and he ducked out as he pulled the stiff canvas cover off his old Springfield. He already had on his leathers tight around his belly.

"Doc," I said, "you don't have to do this."

He grinned at me and tossed the empty cover over the crest of his tent. "Yep, I do. I'm part of this company."

"What about …" I didn't want to mention his weak heart or his fear of having another heart attack. He was a paramedic as well as a patient. He knew the risks. That was why he hadn't gone on the field since his heart attack in Gettysburg.

"I can't let that stop me. I gotta be with the boys." With that, he hefted his musket to his shoulder and headed toward the line of gray figures.

I took my place in the rear rank. Jake was in front, looking pale. He was facing Badger and looked on the verge of pleading with him. I hoped it was to stop this insane exercise. But it wasn't.

"I'm not taking command," Badger was saying.

"But you should. I'm all right if it's just marching around or in a reenactment battle. But this is for real. I don't know what to do."

"Yeah you do, Jake. You're fine."

"Badger, you know what's coming. You'd be better in command than me. I can't do this." He glanced hesitantly at the rest of us.

Badger laid a heavy paw on Jake's shoulder. "Yes, you can. Trust God. You're in command for a reason. You lead us in."

Jake shook his head as Badger took his place at the end of the ranks. He stood in front of us, took a deep breath, and mustered his strength.

"Count off in twos!" he ordered. We did so, though in an uncharacteristic whisper so as not to disturb the rest of the camp. "Shoulder … arms. In ranks, right face. March!"

The mist curled around us and our tents were lost behind us.

Chapter Sixteen

Put on the whole armour of God, that ye may be able to stand against the wiles of the devil ... Ephesians 6:11

The sun must be about to rise, hesitantly peeking over the horizon that lay somewhere in the distance. Where it might be, I couldn't tell, but it was lighter. The mist took on a glow that dissipated the darkness. I couldn't tell east from any other direction. I only hoped that Captain Jake knew his way around the battlefield. I wondered if this was how it appeared a hundred and fifty years earlier before the battle. This was an alien landscape compared to the same hills during the daylight. I would not have been surprised to discover we had been transported to another world or dimension. It would have made more sense than the rest of this weekend.

I recognized the stone wall over which we had retreated on the previous day during our reenactment, and where I may have been transported through time to witness the aftermath of the original battle. My hand slipped into my pocket and felt the little silver cross, but it didn't give me much comfort.

We heard them coming before we saw them.

"Front!" came Jake's command, and we turned in our ranks to face the advancing enemy. "Load and to the shoulder!"

I flipped open my cartridge box and pulled out a paper cartridge. I felt something hard inside, resting on the grains of black powder. I pinched it between my fingers and could determine a solid metal cylindrical shape that came to a point.

"Hey," I heard Sam say, "these cartridges are real. There's Minié balls in them."

A murmur went along our ranks.

"It's okay," Jake said, moving along our front rank. "Rip off the end like always. Pour the powder in, then pinch in the ball. Yeah, that's it. Now use the ramrod to shove it all down. Easy. C'mon, hurry up. Now cap the nipple."

Were they nuts? I didn't like the idea of using live rounds. Why wasn't anyone even questioning why our boxes were filled with real cartridges, bullets and all? The paper didn't even feel like the type I used to roll our cartridges. I glanced on either side of me to see that the others were in various stages of loading, some shoving the rod down the barrel, others pinching the percussion caps onto the nipples. I shook my head and followed suit, determined not to fire, or at least to aim into the ground. What if the advancing troops were really other reenactors out for an early morning drill? Could I stop my friends before they shot into ranks of living, breathing people?

The enemy crested a shallow rise in the field and took form out of the mist.

At first it was a single long mass of blue, rolling over the crest like a huge dark amoeboid oozing over the field. Then they took on individual shapes while the thump-thumping of their feet drew closer. There may have been fifty men in the front rank, with an equal number right behind, marching in perfect formation, weapons at shoulder arms. A hundred men. There were eight of us.

When they topped the crest, a single officer appeared behind them, his sword drawn and raised high. A slouch hat hid his features, but I knew it was the colonel who challenged us. He paused at the hill's crest and I felt him gaze at me and smile. I couldn't see any of this and tried to convince myself it was only my imagination.

We never heard any command from the advancing army. They just stopped as one, the sudden silence rushing in to fill the field. Every rifle shifted to the ready position, then to be aimed.

The blast of one hundred rifles rivaled any cannon I have ever heard, even standing near it. The red flash blazed across the ranks, obliterating the blue figures.

Something whizzed past me.

Sam spun, catching his arm. "Ahh!"

He dropped to his knees, the butt of his musket planted in the grass, his arm wrapped around the rifle for support. His left hand clutched his right shoulder. He gingerly pulled it away and we all saw the blood covering his palm.

"Fall back!" Jake cried.

I grabbed one side of Sam, Daniel took the other, and together we pulled him to his feet and dragged him backwards. I nearly tripped over the stone wall when we came to it, but I managed to step over it without much grace. We got Sam down and Doc scrambled over.

Crouching down behind the wall, I looked over the stones at the blue army. They were now in the process of reloading, shoving cartridges into the breeches of their rifles. I glanced along the wall and was relieved to see Steve near Badger. Everyone was accounted for. Our only casualty had been Sam.

Doc cut the sleeve of Sam's shell jacket, exposing the wound, and cleaned and disinfected it. He had the advantage of modern medical techniques and some modern tools in his haversack.

"The bullet didn't go in," Doc said. "Just cut through the outside of your arm, made a deep furrow."

"Burns like hell," Sam said between clenched teeth.

Doc began wrapping a bandage around Sam's arm. "You'll be fine. I've seen a lot worse."

Sam scowled at him. "Yeah, well this isn't 'Nam. And we aren't soldiers. We're play actors, and those are real bullets."

Another blast echoed across the mist-covered field and bullets whizzed over our heads, punched into the ground, or splintered rocks in the wall.

"I don't think they're reenactors," Daniel pointed out.

"Keep down," Jake said as he hobbled like a frog behind us. "Keep cover behind the wall. Ready, aim!"

Five of us crouched and held our muskets out over the stone wall, taking aim at the opposing wall of blue. I was no longer worried that these might be fellow reenactors, but I still wondered who they might be. And then I looked into the face of one. He was just like the other forty-nine in his rank, and he wasn't human. Shaped like a human, with human features, but not human eyes. Even at this distance I could tell. They were cold, reddish, reptilian, and I nearly froze to the rocks in front of me.

I took careful aim.

"Fire!"

Our volley was not as well executed as any in our drills or on the field, but that was understandable. I felt the heavy kick against my shoulder and saw a puff of dirt a dozen feet in front of my target. Since no one among the enemy fell or stumbled, I guessed none of us had hit anything.

"Reload and to the ready!" Jake called.

The enemy fired again, reloaded, and advanced.

"They've got breech loaders!" Charlie yelled.

"What?" Jake said. He looked over the wall, saber in one hand, Colt in the other. "Good grief, you're right. They're Sharps breech loaders."

Sam groaned. "Now that's just cheating. And I should know."

Doc scrambled up beside me, dragging his musket. Sam winced from the other side of him but brought up his own rifle. Both guns were still loaded from earlier and had yet to be fired. Sam's sweat-soaked face twisted as he brought up his musket and held it ready, leaning its weight against the stones.

"Aim. Fire!"

This time our volley sounded more precise, exploding in one blast. Two figures in blue toppled over, and we all gave up a cheer.

We were reloading when they fired back.

Doc fell against me, nearly knocking me over.

I spun to him, dropping my musket so I could catch him and ease him to the ground. His round face grimaced. Both hands clutched his chest. Blood oozed between his fingers. I lowered him to the ground and crouched over him. What do I do next? He was shot! In the chest. This was impossible. I called to him, but his eyes rolled back.

"Doc! Don't do this!"

I dug into his haversack and pulled out scissors and bottles and packs of bandages. I grabbed one large pack and tore off the wrapping. I pried his hands away and pushed the bandage down onto his chest. The white gauze was immediately lost in the red ooze. I fumbled to tear open more packs. There weren't enough.

His hand wrapped around my wrist, blood sliding between his fingers.

"Frank ..."

"Hang on, Doc. Hang on. We'll get you outta here." I tried to remember my basic first aid. Chest wounds weren't covered in the course. Doc was the expert. He had lived through 'Nam, saved lives, watched men die.

"I don't want to die," he said.

"You're not going to," I said, feeling like I was lying.

Our men fired another volley, and one thundered in reply. Someone cried out and I quickly looked for Steve. He was still next to Badger, pulling the ramrod out of his musket and sliding it back in place. On the other side, Daniel lay on the ground, his arms flailing, his feet pumping to right himself. He must have been hit. But not as bad as Doc.

I pulled free of Doc and lifted up my musket to finish reloading. The blue mass drew closer in steady, strong steps, rifles held at the ready. I took careful aim at one of them and squeezed the trigger. The smoke nearly obliterated my target, but I was able to see one figure stumble and disappear. One from behind stepped up and took his place. Soon they would breach our wall and we'd meet them at the point of the bayonet.

Doc's musket lay nearby. He was loading it when he was hit. I turned to reach for Doc's rifle, but he caught me again.

"Frank ... I'm afraid."

Well, I didn't feel too secure at the moment, either.

They were moving steadily closer. I capped off Doc's Springfield and aimed over the meager rock fortification. Their features were clearer, those reptilian eyes staring, unblinking. Then ... the one I had in my sight was Jeremy, his eyes filled with fear. He was in front of me and now I held the gun on him. I would send the bullet that would rip through his skull and brain.

"No!"

I lowered the rifle and fired into the ground. A puff of dirt blew up from the impact.

"It wasn't my fault!" Steve had been right. Jeremy had problems. I may have stopped him from hurting anyone else, but it wasn't my fault he took his own life. That had been his choice. We all have choices.

I looked out across the field through the smoke and mist at the men approaching.

No, they weren't men. This wasn't a real battle.

"Fix bayonets!" Jake called.

On either side of me, my friends slid bayonets from their scabbards and twisted them into place on the ends of their muskets. I reached for mine but stopped.

This wasn't a real battle.

I was a science teacher. Doc was a restaurant owner. Jake was a mailman. Steve was a student.

But Doc was lying there facing his death, just like in his dream. His fear of dying. Glancing at the others, I saw the fear in their eyes.

This *was* a real battle. But those weren't men.

I remembered what Badger had said. We weren't fighting flesh and blood. These weren't men. They were demons, disguised, playing with us, playing on our fears. And we weren't going to defeat them with bullets and bayonets. What was the rest of that passage? "For we wrestle not against flesh and blood, but against principalities, against powers, against rulers of the darkness of this world, against spiritual wickedness in high places." But there was more! How do you fight them?

I spoke the verses as though I knew them, but though I remembered the words I didn't remember committing them to memory.

"'Wherefore take unto you the whole armor of God, that ye may be able to withstand in the evil day, and having done all, to stand.'"

I stood up, leaving Doc's musket leaning against the rock wall.

"'Stand, therefore, having girt about with truth, and having on the breastplate of righteousness;

"'And your feet shod with the preparation of the gospel of peace;

"'Above all, taking the shield of faith, wherewith ye shall be able to quench all the fiery darts of the wicked.'"

A volley exploded from across the field. Bullets whizzed through the air, but I felt none strike.

I continued reciting, my voice echoing over the battlefield. "'And take the helmet of salvation, and the sword of the spirit, which is the word of God.'"

"Frank!" Jake hissed. "Get down."

I looked over at him cowering behind the wall, filled with fear. His sword was up and he was ready to lead his men into the jaws of the enemy, only this wasn't an earthly enemy. They didn't fight fair. They were part of a spiritual world that coexisted with ours, not filled with ghosts but with other kinds of spirits. I never could believe in ghosts, because they weren't real. These other spirits were.

"No," I said to Jake. "We can't win with muskets. Don't you understand? Badger, you're the one who first said it. These aren't Union troops and we aren't Confederates. Two days ago you were working in your motorcycle shop. Jake, you were delivering mail. These are demons. They aren't men. We can't kill them."

Jake slashed the air with his saber. "Just look at Doc. Look at that wound, Frank, and tell me that's not real."

I bent down to Doc and placed my hand over the hole burnt in his chest, felt the sticky blood between my finger. Beneath, his heart feebly pumped. Was the wound real? It felt real. This was blood. I could smell the blood, feel it. His heart was failing him. His heart ...

"Doc, listen to me. I think you're having a heart attack. You've been through this before and came out okay. Just hang in there."

"Frank ... I'm afraid ... of dying."

"Don't be. Have faith."

"Don't know where I'm ... going."

"Then make sure," I told him. "Right now. You've heard Badger talk about his salvation. You've heard it before, you just never accepted it. Right now, Doc. You just ask God to forgive you, accept him into your heart, accept his salvation. The helmet of salvation. That's how we beat these things, with the sword of God, not with bayonets."

"Pray?" he asked.

"No. Talk to God like you do to me. Now."

He did, then laid his head back. He was still pale, but the tightness had left his face. His breathing was still rapid, but the corners of his lips curled up. The fear had gone.

I jumped back up.

They were almost on us but the others had been watching Doc and me and not our enemy. Even Daniel, lying on the ground, had propped himself on an elbow to see and listen.

"Doc was afraid of dying," I said. "Badger, you're afraid of your past. Jake, you're afraid of ... that you can't be a leader. Daniel, you're afraid you turned your back on your heritage. Steve, you ... you're afraid of what's going to happen when you leave home. Sam, Charlie ... Don't you guys see? They're working on our fears. You can't fight them this way."

Badger lowered his head, then shook it. Then he gently placed his musket on the ground and stood up.

"He's right. We can't fight 'em like this. We gotta use faith. Only God can defeat them."

"It doesn't make sense," Jake said, gripping his saber tighter, hefting it. "Those ... things ... are shooting at us."

Badger puffed up his barrel chest and grinned. "And only the shield of faith'll protect us. And the helmet of salvation."

The next volley ripped through us with a thunder so loud it stung my ears.

Jake's eyes widened. Had that been a real volley, Badger and I would have been ripped to pieces. Slowly, he turned his saber, guided the tip to the scabbard, and then slid it in. He unbuckled the scabbard from his belt and laid it on the stone wall. He glanced up at Badger. "Sword of the spirit?"

"Yep. 'Which is the word of God,'" Badger said.

Jake undid two buttons on his sack coat and slid his hand inside. When he withdrew his hand he held a small book. "I keep it in there, just like the original soldiers did. It used to be just part of the impression. It's been years since I've read it."

Badger dug into his haversack and pulled out an identical book.

Steve stood and came to stand beside me.

Jake stood up next to Badger.

Daniel winced and pushed himself up. Sam and Charlie helped him the rest of the way.

"The shield of faith, boys!" Jake shouted.

"The breastplate of righteousness," Badger said.

"The helmet of salvation," came Doc's weakened voice, almost a croak, but tinged with a strength of assurance.

"And the sword of the spirit," Jake said as he held up his little Bible as he would have his saber.

The blue figures seemed more than a hundred in number now, forming a double line that curved toward the little wall which had been our meager protection. For a moment I thought of that vision of this battlefield littered with bodies and imagined the eight of us lying among them. Whether I had hallucinated or actually traveled back, it didn't matter. The men who died here a hundred and fifty years ago had faced other men, not these creatures. This was not the same battle.

The sun must have been rising over the horizon behind us, for a faint glow slowly illuminated the enemy as they edged closer to us. Their reddish eyes widened and they stopped as one with a mere twenty feet between us.

I heard a sound behind us as though a hundred swords scraped against their scabbards as they were drawn.

I wanted to turn, to see the origin of the sound, but all I could do was watch the faces of these beings before us, things that pretended to be men out of history. In a moment, the smooth young faces filled with fear and the thin veneer of humanity fled like vapor and I could see the disfigured ugliness that had lain beneath. Before I could feel any revulsion, blazing light flooded the field as though the sun not only rose to its fullness but suddenly went nova in that instance.

A tidal wave of brilliance rushed past us and into the frozen army.

I felt the hot breeze on my face, heard the flutter of wings, and saw a brightness that blotted out everything else, and for a moment I thought I could see bright figures holding blazing swords. One paused and turned to me for the briefest of moments, a mere heartbeat, and I saw a handsome golden face smile at me.

And then we were alone on the Pine Creek battlefield, wisps of mist curling over the ground.

Chapter Seventeen

Now faith is the substance of things hoped for, the evidence of things not seen … Hebrews 11:1

The seven of us, dressed in soiled wool uniforms, smelling of black powder, smoke, and perspiration, crowded into the hospital room. There was no sneaking in, with the clip-clop of the metal plates on our brogans striking the tile floor. The nurses put up a fuss but we ignored them. After all, we had just faced an army of demons. What was a handful of nurses and hospital security? Nothing was about to chase us away from spending just one minute in that room. We huddled together, our collective aroma staggering, surrounded by the beeps of the monitoring equipment. The figure on the bed stirred.

"I know I'm not dead," Doc's weak voice said, barely above the ambient instrument noise. "I know now where I'm headed, I just don't know about the rest of you."

He lifted his head to look at his chest covered by the blue gown and a few layers of sheets. Wires wound around his pillow and disappeared down the v-neck of the hospital gown, terminating somewhere in electrodes taped to his chest.

"I guess I wasn't shot."

"Nope," Jake said. "Heart attack."

"Could've sworn ..." Doc began, then his voice trailed off.

"Yeah," Sam said, "me too." He lifted his arm a few times, like a bird testing its wing. Then he stuck his finger into the torn shirt, probing the flesh of his arm. The green cloth of the shirt was dirty, but it had no bloodstain. "Remember? You even bandaged it. You cut the sleeve off my shell jacket. And it sure felt like I was shot. I can still remember the pain."

"I was shot, too," Daniel said. He jabbed his fingers into the middle of his stomach. "Right here. And it still feels sore, but there's no wound."

"So," Doc said, his brow furrowing, "it wasn't real. I thought maybe I dreamt the whole thing. Did I?"

I shook my head. "No, it was real, sort of. It wasn't part of the physical world. We were actually in a spiritual world, like a parallel universe. But not."

Doc rolled his eyes. "This from a scientist."

"Don't matter none," Badger said. "It was real enough to us and you could've died for real. I don't know what would have happened if they had overrun us. They were deceivers and they were trying to trick us the whole time. They were from the father of lies. But we beat 'em. With a little help." He pointed his finger toward the ceiling.

"A lot of help," I said.

"Wouldn't have thought a scientist would come up with the idea of using faith instead of some solid, tangible weapon," Doc said. His voice seemed to gain some strength, though his throat must have been dry. He kept licking his cracked lips. I found a cup with a little bit of ice still in the water and held it over for him to reach the straw.

"There are more things in this world, Horatio," I said, butchering Shakespeare.

A voice hissed from behind us. "I will tell all of you one last time, leave! This patient needs rest and there is a limit to visitors. Out!"

We filed past Doc as we left, and his fingers curled over my arm to hold me behind while the others cleared the room.

"Frank, thanks. I'm not afraid of dying. I'm not ready for it to happen today, but it doesn't scare me. In a way, I look forward to it. But I'm still not in a hurry. I've got a few things to learn, first." He motioned to the Gideon Bible on the stand next to the bed.

"What about you," he asked, "do you think you're free of your ghost?"

For a moment I wondered if he meant the colonel. I doubted I would ever see that person again, though maybe he would try some other tactic in some other disguise. But Doc meant the other apparition that haunted me.

"I don't think so," I told him. "I may never be free of him, but I know it wasn't my fault. It was a tragedy and it was out of my control. Maybe somewhere down the line he'll help me help other kids."

"Still giving up teaching?"

"No. There's too much work to do. Too many kids. Now get some rest."

He was asleep before I stepped out of the room.

Outside, Jake leaned against the wall next to the door.

"He's going to be all right," he said.

"Yep."

"Me, too."

"Good," I said. "Where is everyone?"

He nodded down the hall. "In the waiting room. You guys go on back to camp. I'll stay here with Doc."

I wasn't entirely willing to desert Doc, but I did want to clean up. "Are you sure?"

"Yeah." He gave a small grin. "It's the least his commanding officer could do." The smile faded and his features took on a more serious expression. "He's my responsibility. I need to stay with him probably more than he needs me here. I'm not leaving until he does. Anyway, someone has to drive him back. He's not going to be able to do that himself."

"Tell you what," I said, "we'll pack up your things, load your truck, and bring you your civilian clothes. I doubt you want to wait around here dressed like that. Maybe there's a room at the motel. I'll get Daniel to check on it. You need a shower."

"So do you," he said, grinning again. "Thanks. That'll be great."

I walked out into the waiting area where the others were scattered around. I passed Charlie first, where he was hunched over his cell phone. I overheard him talking to his wife, telling her he would be on his way home soon, in time to take her out to dinner. He gave me a wink as I went by. Daniel was talking with a young nurse, discussing politics. She was a pretty girl with mocha skin, and she nodded along with Daniel, agreeing with what he said. Two kindred spirits. Badger and Sam were talking. Sam held his pack of playing cards in one hand.

"So Badger—" Sam was saying.

Badger held up a finger to interrupt him. "Name's Graham. Not Badger."

"So, I was just saying, I don't need these anymore. Don't even have the urge. It feels real good." He twisted and shot the pack through the air like a basketball. It dropped into a wastebasket next to the vending machine.

And Steve was with Jenna. She handed him a computer flash drive, then gave him a hug. The hug lasted a bit too long and finished up with a kiss that was a bit more than a plutonic peck. When she hurried off, Steve came over to me. His cheeks were flushed and his eyes were directed toward his feet.

"She, ah, wanted to drop this off before she went back home, back to her dad's." He lifted the flash drive, pinched between finger and thumb. "It's Captain Long's journal. She scanned it this morning, before she took it back to Mrs. Letterman. She wants me to do an article on it, maybe try to get it published. Her grandfather won't like it, but she doesn't care. He's already trying to buy the journal from Mrs. Letterman, but she won't sell. Jenna said she's sick over what really happened, now that she knows what's in the journal. She has some letters for me to see if I want to write up something. Maybe I'll do a doctorate thesis on it."

"Doctorate?" I said, trying to calculate the cost of all those years of college.

"It may not make any difference, but Jenna and I, and Mrs. Letterman, want the truth to get out there."

"You aren't serious about Jenna, are you?" I asked hesitantly.

"Jenna?" His face reddened more. "She's nice. But we're just friends. We don't even live in the same town."

"Ready to go home?" I felt as though I had been up all weekend.

"Yeah. I got a lot to do before leaving for school."

As we walked back toward the others I slung my arm over his shoulders. "So, college isn't so intimidating?"

"Naw. Can't wait to get started. Besides, next year Jenna will be going. She wants to be a history teacher, too. She's applying to the same college, and with her grades and her dad being a lawyer, she won't have any trouble getting in."

"Same college?" I asked, stunned.

"Yep."

"Now I'm worried," I said.

"Aw, Dad! Have a little faith."

THE END

About Our Creators

AUTHOR –

WAYNE CAREY - A life-long fan of science fiction and pulp fiction, Wayne Carey grew up reading Edgar Rice Burroughs, H.G. Wells, Isaac Asimov, H. Rider Haggard and all the grand masters, which guided him toward a career in science with degrees in biology and education and provided the desire to write from an early age. A love of classic and noire films, such as Casablanca and The Maltese Falcon, also influences his writing. He is the author of The Nanon Factor, a young adult contemporary science fiction thriller that blends a murder mystery with cutting edge technology, and has appeared in a variety of anthologies such as Legends of New Pulp Fiction. He and his wife Brenda live in the wilds of Central Pennsylvania with their three children, who provide a great deal of inspiration for his work. Email him at wgcarey@1791.com.

INTERIOR ILLUSTRATOR –

ED CATTO - A voracious reader, Ed has been enjoying pulps since stumbling across Shadow and Doc Savage reprints as a kid. His love for illustration and art has guided him through a life-long love of comics, pulps and illustrated paperbacks. As a branding and advertising executive, Ed's career has evolved to include a focus on entertainment marketing in many ways:

A founding partner of Bonfire Agency, Ed helped establish the world's first marketing firm focused on connecting brands, in authentic ways, to passionate and enthusiastic fans of comics, graphic novels, games and movies.

Ed has also shepherded the rebirth of the iconic 60s toy, Captain Action, in collectibles, books, comics and even a national toy line. An animated television series is currently being shopped for development.

A convention enthusiast, Ed helped develop Reed Pop's New York

Comic-Con (now the nation's largest con) and is currently doing the same for Syracuse's Salt City Comic-Con.

Ed speaks nationally as a panelist and moderator at conventions, leading conversations on entertainment marketing and comics history. Ed has also appeared on CNBC's Squawkbox, BNN Business News Network, and PBS's Superheroes documentary.

Ed recently started teaching at Ithaca College, sharing his experiences and enthusiasm for business and entrepreneurship to both MBA's and undergraduates. As an artist, Ed also leads graphic novel classes for kids of all ages. *The Adventures of Captain Graves* marked Ed's debut as an illustrator for publisher Airship27. Ed and his wife Kathe currently live in New York's State's Finger Lakes Region, enjoying the area's local comic book shops and wineries. Between consulting, teaching and drawing, Ed continues to work very hard to whittle down the teetering tower of books on his nightstand.

COVER ARTIST –

LAURA GIVENS is a Denver Based author and artist. Her art has graced the covers of numerous publishers' books and may be viewed at www.lauragivens-artist.com . In 2010 she naively decided she could write stories as well many she had illustrated. She has sold ten to date including the story in this volume. She was co-editor and contributor to Six-Guns Straight From Hell, a weird western anthology recently released. She performed improv comedy on stage for a decade then produced, wrote, directed and filmed her no-budget masterpiece, The Jerusalem Tango, which you will never see for good cause—trust me.